DEAD

RIVER

M°CAID
PAUL

Audience: Ages 13+ | Summary: After seventeen-year-old Clayton Thomas discovers a dead body along the riverbank and a strange girl living alone in a houseboat, he soon learns trusting a stranger is his only chance for survival.

Cover Illustration and book formatting by © 2023 Damonza
Edited by Josh Vogt
Author Photo by Amanda Bosenberg
eBook ISBN: 978-1-7357299-5-4
Paperback ISBN: 978-1-7357299-6-1
Hardcover ISBN: 978-1-7357299-7-8

DEAD

RIVER

To my parents, as always

And Watt Key, whose stories inspired me to write my own

1

WHITE-SKINNED CREATURE

'M A MILE out from the boat landing when I notice the yellow police tape fluttering in the breeze. Evidence of what happened here less than a month ago: a girl's corpse found on the banks, bloated from days in the river, a logging chain laced around her ankles to weigh her down. The paper said she was my age, late teens. Her broken fingernails, lacerations, and chipped teeth proved that she hadn't gone down without a fight.

I'd heard the rumors, subjected to the hearsay a month ago when school was in session, all the lies teens tell in order to gain a leg up in the ladder of status and gossip. Some guys in my junior class claimed the girl was a prostitute who became involved with the wrong crowd, the wrong client. Others hinted that she was a drifter—someone who never stays in one place for too long.

I know the type.

Either way, it came as no surprise that as soon as the grisly murder hit the local press, the tragedy was the biggest news in the region. The story spanned miles, whispered about over steaming mugs of black coffee served several miles north of the Choctawhatchee at Delton Café—a place with more old men than menu items—and floated around the last month of school like the odor of burning hemp, encroaching and foul.

It also came as no surprise that instead of staying far, far away from the scene of the crime, residents flocked to it, bringing with them teddy bears, bouquets of white orchids, and half-used candles, devoting a shrine of forgotten items to a lost girl.

This morning, the scene is mostly submerged, several flower petals floating across the river's calm surface. They're the only sign that a girl's screams stood no defense against the remoteness of the river-fed swampland.

Homicides happen too often along the Choctawhatchee, but not often enough for the news to grow stale or for people to simply gawk and move on. The misfortunes fester for several weeks, until one day they're reduced to several bolded words in a newspaper that no one reads. Forever a statistic. Forever a tragedy.

Thirty-two. According to Google, that's how many documented bodies have been found along the river through the years. Most of them are runaways—females barely out of high school. Others are unidentifiable, with no information in the database to link a name or face to the victim. Girls who—depending on those you asked—had it coming.

Their cases are rarely solved.

Overnight, the river level rose three feet. The culprit: two inches of rain three days ago in South Alabama. Now, the usual pale-gray water resembles a coffee brown, tainted with a hint of orange from the clay hills along the river. Shadows stretch across the muddy current. Brambles, vines, and palmettos rustle in the wind from the shore. In a couple hours, the June heat will become unbearable, the water level will begin to recede, and the harsh sun will pound down on the river until its surface glistens like fish scales.

It's been an hour without sign of other fishermen or boats roaring past. This is typical. No one comes here as often as I do.

My aluminum, twelve-foot Jon boat picks up speed, wind tousling my brown hair, as I tear my gaze away from the all-too familiar crime scene. Most days, it's a side glance in passing, a sight I've come to expect, like the looming cypress trees with knotted roots on either side of the bank or flocks of waterfowl resting in the overhead branches. Sometimes, like today, I can't help but stare a second too long, drawn by the recollection of the black-and-white crime scene photos printed across the front page of *The Delton Times*, forever burned in my memory.

Five miles from the landing, near a checkpoint known on my map as Hidden Creek, a strange sensation works its way down my spine, my palms tingling and the back of my neck prickling. It's second nature to me now—this feeling of being watched. Maybe it's due to the memorial of a dead girl or the thought that a killer still hasn't been caught. Maybe it's some subconscious alertness to nature. Whatever the cause, I've discovered that I can't overlook it.

The feeling sharpens as I slow my skiff at the base of a leaning tree, cypress knees surrounding the area like a sacred fortress. Hairs rise on the nape of my neck, a rivulet of sweat tracing my backbone.

Get a grip, Clayton, I tell myself. *You're just being paranoid.*

Slivers of light sneak down through the overhead branches. It's just past sunrise, and all around are the echoes of the swamp: a bream slapping the surface of the water, bullfrogs croaking from the sandy-white banks, and an anhinga fluttering its wings at the edge of the tree line. A blue heron watches from the shore, still as a statue, its neck curved into a tight *S* shape. A turtle sits perched on the edge of a log, head raised like a dog awaiting its next command. Occasionally, on mornings like this, I'm lucky enough to spot an alligator or a beaver splashing about near the bank.

Sometimes, when the air is nippy and a blanket of fog hovers above the water's surface, I can't help but think of Dad. Whether teaching me to tie bush hooks on branches along the shore using a special knot or tending to the bow line while he parked the truck, Dad was someone I could always count on to keep me focused. My dad was a man who handled everything with a careful ease, who never cursed or screamed, even that time our fuse blew and we floated downstream for what seemed like half a day, trying to find our way back. He was a man of high optimism—one who had me fooled from a young age that nothing could ever go wrong in his presence, in the safety and confines of our Jon boat.

Aside from his tranquil demeanor and his laser-like concentration, Dad also religiously kept a pistol stored in an old tackle box in the bow of the boat. *It's a precaution, Clay,* he'd told me once—a habit I sure wish I would've inherited.

I've read the stories. I've heard the legends. And one thing I've never understood in all my time exploring these sloughs and the river's never-ending network of cutoffs is why the area seems like such a good place for internment—confined and guarded by the canopy of towering cypress trees. From as much as I've seen on shows like *Dateline* and *Forensic Files*, bodies on the river never stay hidden for long.

Perhaps my unease is rooted in the past, in the story of the girl who was lost to these waters less than a month ago, this feeling chalked up to a bit of healthy paranoia, given the history of this place.

Shaking it off, I continue on my way.

Several yards ahead, a catfish bobs in the swift stream, caught on a bush hook set the day before. On instinct, I reach one hand into the tepid water until my fingers brush against nylon, my other hand enclosing around the fish's slippery head to prevent its ice pick-like spines from sticking into my skin. After lifting the channel cat out into the light, I give several reverse tugs to pull the hook from its mouth, pressing down hard enough to keep the fish from thrashing. It's about five to six pounds, if I had to guess. I can easily make $9. $12 if I get lucky.

Retrieving the hook, I open the live well and toss the fish inside, listening to the bumping of the channel cat against the side of the metal box. *Nice sized one,* Dad would say.

A black nylon line tied just the exact way and 2/0 hooks so sharp they could pierce through any meaty bait are just the right recipe to catch a catfish. It began as a hobby of mine. Now, it's more of a job. I catch the fish, sell them by the pound, and skin them for an extra charge. Locals would be surprised how much I can rack up in a month. Competition is slim. Hardly anyone knows this place exists, which adds to my luck.

It isn't called Hidden Creek for nothing.

Sure, it can be hard work sometimes, with the sweltering, muggy heat and mosquitoes which seem as big as dragonflies, or the nights of a storm, when it's nearly impossible to navigate across the rushing stream through the stinging rain to find the last hook. But that's just life on the Choctawhatchee. I wouldn't have it any other way. The river is a part of me—all I know and all I can fall back on when things don't turn out like I want them to.

For instance, Dad's diagnosis. Month after month of chemotherapy and radiation. So many promises made within that short time, but so many unkept.

Terminal, the doctor said—something that couldn't be stopped. At the time, I wasn't sure if I believed it. But then there were the days Dad could hardly walk, conversations reduced to a few words, as if the sounds required too much effort. In the beginning, I'd hoped that he would slowly build back his strength—that one day, he'd have enough energy to walk a mile, go fishing again in our boat, or be able to feel the sunlight on his face, the dirt between his toes.

But now he's gone, just like my mother, whose heels click-clacked down the walk at six years old, right out of my life. Gone like my grandpa, who taught me how to shoot my first rifle, but now can't seem to even remember my name.

Out here, miles from civilization, in a habitat much different from home, it's easy pretending to be someone else. Someone untouched by pain and the chaos of cancer, unfamiliar with the cruel spiral of dementia and the murky faces of those from my past, like the blotchy spots on an old photograph.

Out here, it's easy to forget.

With the catfish in the live well, I retrieve the bait in an icebox beneath my seat, plucking a striped Catawba worm from the square metal cage. The worm writhes in my white-knuckled grip, trying to wiggle free, but I'm too quick, piercing its tough skin with a sharp 2/0 hook. Yellow liquid drips from my fingers, sliding down the metal shank as a strong musky smell fills the air.

Catawba worms are typically only used for my smaller lines, whereas pieces of mullet are used in their place for the larger ones. On top of my other job at Bart's Bait 'N Tackle shop, I've developed a market for catfish within the past year with certain locals—particularly older women in town like Ms. Judy—who call every week to see what I've caught. *Got any big ones for me, Clay?* Ms. Judy always asks. *You know how much I love those filets.*

After setting my line, I power on my 9.9 HP Johnson Outboard engine, slipping away to the next hook several yards down the river.

On the far side of the bank lies a white-skinned creature, caught between tree roots and gnarled limbs like a fish in a net. It's probably just an animal—a large fish or a bloated deer.

But then I catch sight of what looks like the head of an old mop, twisted around the roots and streaked with mud.

Hair. It's hair.

I blink, the image sharpening, growing clearer. The pale white of a belly, two sets of fingers extending out, and the gaping hole of an open mouth, caught in a silent scream.

It's a body.

2

CARCASS

TIME STANDS STILL as I edge closer.

Articles of clothing hang from the woman's limbs in awkward positions—a denim skirt hugging her knees, a black bra clinging to her ribs.

Flies hover above, so many I'm afraid that if I breathe, I'll suck one in.

Powering off my trolling motor, I gather my rope from the floor of the boat and tie it around a stump a couple of feet away from the corpse, which has swelled beyond recognition at this point.

Something black trails down the woman's cheek. For a second, I almost mistake it for a long line of mascara. But then I take a step closer, my feet meeting solid ground.

My lungs constrict as I realize. Ants, too many to count, march down her pale, bare skin and into her open mouth, then back out and up to one wide, unblinking eye.

The other is closed, swollen shut, so purple I can't help but wonder if the eyeball would bulge right out if she happened to blink.

Something moves behind the lid, poking its way out and squirming free—a red-headed beetle. It's followed by a short body, tiny legs scuttling into the light.

Now, only inches away, I'm choked by the smell, so cloying it's difficult to breathe. I place a hand over my mouth, turning away and pinching my eyes shut, like somehow that'll block out the scent, a culmination of the gases leaving the body.

It's like a hundred different odors all at once. Rotting cabbage. Eggs. Rancid garlic.

My nose burns at the fumes, heart bucking in my chest, as a sound begins at the base of my throat, racing up.

The spray of vomit. My hacking coughs as I sputter for air.

I can't get away fast enough.

In my drunken-like stagger, my foot catches on a root and I fall. Pain slices through my palms and my calves, but still my throat continues pumping the vile mess out of my stomach. Once it's done, I can't help but heave just thinking about the smell.

It's in my clothes. It's in my skin. The barbaric, primitive side of me can't get behind the thought that I'm breathing in another human's gas. My tongue feels violated and slick with the nasty aroma, and I want to scrub it until it's raw, until the taste is gone. I might not ever be able to get it clean again.

I'd always heard that a body in the water—otherwise known as a floater—was like a carcass pumped full of air, and once I'm brave enough to look back at the woman, I can't help but mistake her for anything other than a bloated mannequin. Anything human is gone.

Wiping the last grainy flecks of vomit from my chin, I snatch the rope out from around the stump, place the gear shift in neutral, and turn the key. The engine roars to life.

For an instant, my thoughts return to Dad. Right now, I wish he was here; wish I could wrap my arms around his chest and hear his calm whisper in my ear.

Everything will be okay. Don't be scared, Clay.

I can't help but wonder: *What would Dad do?*

Would he turn and scream, mumble a curse, or call the police, frantic and scared, like I am now?

If only I had that gun. If only I was just a little more like the man I knew Dad to be.

It's not real, Clayton, a voice tells me. *Only something you've imagined.*

My hands tremble, and I resist the urge to scream. I can't help but stare at the human carcass along the bank, an image that'll be ingrained forever in my mind, burned behind my eyelids.

It's so unreal that, for a moment, it seems too unfortunate to be anything other than a flicker of my imagination; a stroke of color across canvas, conjuring the body and its surroundings into being, like a painting of something tragic. I don't want to accept it, just like I didn't want to accept seeing Dad for the first time in his casket, limp and pallid and ashen. The mere thought of death seems to paralyze me ever since I lost him. It's as if my brain has tried to build a wall to protect my heart while my mind fights back with facts, evidence…with truth.

But then there's the smell and the flies and the underlying sense that someone's watching, that I'm not the only one here. It *is* real.

What's even worse is that, for one fleeting second, I almost thought the woman looked familiar.

I wait until I'm back at the landing to call 911. Maybe here I'll have reception.

Digging the phone from my jean pocket, I quickly type in my five-digit passcode. But before I dial the number, I come to my senses.

I can't get involved with the police. Not again. Last time I was lucky enough to get by with only a ticket.

It was over a year ago, but I can still remember that day almost better than any other. At the time, I'd barely had my driver's license two months when I noticed my "friend" walking home alone, a paper bag tucked under his arm. For some reason, I had the good moral sense to give him a ride home. Little did I know that the bag the guy set in my truck floorboard had two bottles of Jack Daniels and that a Sheriff's Deputy would pull me over for going ten over the speed limit before I could drop him off. I'd barely parked on the edge of the road before the asshole opened the passenger side door and ran like hell for the woods, leaving the opened whiskey on my passenger seat, in plain sight.

Either the cop didn't notice or he just didn't feel like chasing him because I was the one to take the fall for a minor possession of alcohol charge. I can still recall the metal cuffs digging into my wrists and the deputy slamming the car door in my face as I cursed myself in the back of his cruiser, making up my mind to never trust one of my "friends" again.

I haven't spoken to the guy since or any of his drunk-ass buddies. Guys who used to be my friends, too, before I realized they were all the same. Now, I place my trust in the river, and nothing else.

This, after all, is different. We're likely talking foul play. Although, based on my record, I'm not convinced that the police will believe any word I say. I can't deal with this right now anyway, don't want to get mixed up with the cops again. Somebody else fishing these waters will come along and find her. Let them take the heat.

Besides, I've heard people around school refer to me as an average Joe, and I guess they're right. I'm nothing much to look at, if we're being honest—just another skinny, freckle-faced, lanky-legged guy with a mop of brown hair. Trusting the police will do the right thing might just lead me straight into a jail cell, and no one would even blink twice.

Also, everyone in Delton knows the cops are lazy assholes who aren't particularly fond of the media attention whenever another body is found. We've all heard about that reporter they ran off once she started asking too many questions about the last girl. They'll most likely try and sweep this woman's case under the rug, too.

With a sigh, I power off my phone, watching the screen go black. It might be selfish, but it's for the best.

You're crazy. You don't know what you saw.

The thoughts linger, clawing at the inside of my skull, even as I pull the boat onto the trailer, winching it tight, and drive out of the lot without any trace of what I'd seen moments before, other than the smell permeating from my clothes.

I swallow, lick my lips, and turn the radio on, hoping the music will serve as some sort of distraction.

My hands tremble on the wheel and my heart drums, blood pounding in my ears like the heavy bass blasting out of the speakers.

My shift doesn't begin for another couple hours. Still. That's plenty of time to rush back home and take a shower, washing away the scent of her. All the time I need to convince myself what I saw back there wasn't real, only something my tired mind had imagined, given the fresh fear of finding a girl like the one in the papers, bloated beyond recognition.

And the presence I felt, the uncanny sense that someone had been there, watching as I uncovered the body…what was that, exactly?

I sure don't know. And as strange as it sounds, I don't think I want to.

3

A NATURAL BEAST

AFTER **I** **PARK** my F-150 truck in the drive—my panic now a low simmer, even though adrenaline still rushes through my veins—I hurry up the walk, fumble for my keys, and stab the metal into the lock. Cool air rushes out as I step across the threshold.

I can never prepare myself for what I might see on the other side of this door. Some days it's as if nothing's changed, a special kind of normal. My grandpa will be smiling back from the sofa or calling out to me from the kitchen, the space infused with the aroma of onions, garlic, and sizzling meat. Other days, I'm lucky if I get so much as a smile or welcome of any kind.

This morning, I should know better. The house pulses with the sound of appliances—the rhythmic tick of the clock, the hum of the fridge—otherwise undisturbed by my presence.

It's easy to overlook the man sitting in his recliner in a

corner of the living room, quiet and still. He's not asleep, but his eyes are open, staring at the wall. "Good morning," I tell him.

Grandpa doesn't respond.

Most mornings, well after I've checked my hooks, he's usually milling about, pills rattling within their container as he shakes a couple into his hand. In the past, you could say I managed to keep the peace—Grandpa's always had a problem with being cared for—but lately it's like he doesn't even notice me. And when he does, it's typically followed by a story that I've heard a million times.

I try a different approach. "Have you taken your medicine?"

Grandpa turns to look at me but doesn't answer my question. His stare is glassy, and his furry white eyebrows twitch.

"Grandpa, have you taken your medicine?" I ask again, louder.

After several seconds, Grandpa reaches a pale, veiny hand into his trouser pocket, removing a brown medicine bottle. "Count them out for me," he whispers, so soft I barely hear him.

I do as he says, counting out the pills, handing them back, and fetching him an orange Gatorade from the fridge.

"Here," I say, placing the drink on the coffee table next to his recliner. "Do you need anything else?"

No answer.

Forget it, I think, turning on my heel with a sigh.

After all, I have bigger things to worry about right now.

Like the body.

Like the fact that I couldn't even work up the nerve to call the police.

Since Dad's passing, the silence of the house doesn't help. If anything, it only adds to my anxiety.

Dad's door is cracked when I pass in the hall. Fingers enclosing around the doorknob to his room, I manage a quick peek inside. *One look,* I tell myself. *One look won't hurt.*

I blink, and the images sharpen: an alarm clock on his nightstand coated with a fine layer of dust; a basket full of unwashed clothes lying by the foot of his bed, which I imagine still smell like soil and pine; the ruffled white sheets, still unmade from the last time he lay beneath them. I imagine those sheets lifting with the rise and fall of his chest, both feet hanging several inches out from underneath at the end of the queen-sized bed, never enough room for him, especially back when Mom was still around.

Then, the recollection of those early mornings when I'd jump in that space between them, safe and secure with both halves of my world on either side. The sweet fragrance of Mom's hair as I looped several strands around my fingers and Dad's unruly bedhead of brown curls brushing the tips of his lashes as he flashed a sleepy grin—memories that ought to spur a smile on my face instead of a hard lump in my throat.

I count once, twice, before I decide I've seen enough.

I click the door shut and slip away up the padded stairs to my room. It's a habit of mine now. My only way to check that his ghost still exists here, that his memory lives on.

Back then, on the nights when I felt especially brave, I'd creep inside and sit on the edge of the bed, watching him breathe, timing and keeping count of his snores for what felt like hours. If Dad noticed, he never said anything. If he cared, he never admitted it. To me, in his final days, Dad was a ticking time bomb, bound to blow at any given moment.

Dad's oncologist, Dr. Flynn, told me anything was possible, but his eyes spoke different words, the twitch of his mouth and fingers suggesting he'd already nailed the art of the lie. He even had the nerve to smile, a lame attempt to comfort me given the circumstances.

I didn't cry; didn't curse or lift a finger in Flynn's face out of frustration or anger like he probably expected. Instead, I pleaded for a cure, asked for a miracle, even if his response included the same old bull, constructed from the same old logic: *things will get worse before they get better.*

Then and there, I decided I'd had enough of the doctors and professionals who believe they own the world all because of a few degrees, people in fancy white coats which always reek of cleanser—something so strong and sharp that I wonder whether they ever shower to rid themselves of the smell.

Up the stairs, my thoughts drift to someone else, a woman who used to wait at the bottom of these steps, arms wide so I could jump into them, always knocking her back in the process. A woman who kissed the top of my head before bed and tickled my stomach until I lost my breath.

She no longer paces the halls in the middle of the night, hunched over the kitchen counter, silently sobbing into her fist whenever she thinks I'm asleep. But her ghost lives here, too.

I think of her every time I hear the click-clack of high heels and slamming doors. I think of her every time I see the face of a missing person plastered across a telephone pole, half-expecting to recognize the grinning teeth and set of eyes staring back.

My mother left when I was six, which means I haven't heard from her in eleven years. After so many days without a person, you'd think the sting of their absence would lessen, emptiness succumbing to acceptance. Instead of feeling depressed or confused or any other typical emotion that is associated with losing a loved one, what I feel is white-hot anger.

Anger that she left us. Anger that she couldn't even show up to Dad's funeral or bother to call to tell me she was sorry. Anger that—for eleven years of my existence—she chose a life that didn't include me.

After showering and changing into a Guy Harvey T-shirt, faded blue jeans, and a weathered Mojo cap, I'm off to Bart's Bait 'N Tackle. The shop sits on the backside of an old dog track, now abandoned due to Florida voters' sympathy for the hounds. Less than a mile away, through the dense river jungle of oaks, palmettos, and cypress, lies the Choctawhatchee, a source of comfort and a glimpse of home. It's only natural that I built my entire life around the place. It's all I've known since Dad first took me out in his boat, the muddy water rocking, lapping against the shore, stretching as far as the eye could see.

Through my truck windows, I catch occasional glimpses of the river's dark depths and tangled terrain. It's like a whole new world out there, like some undiscovered domain.

Five years old and listening to Dad's words, casting my line into the water and anticipating the first nibble, that first chance of fate. The butter cat, hooked at the end, so heavy that it took both of us to lift him into the boat. That was all it took to make the river feel like something I could rely on, the weight on the end of the line like a promise, like a secret that only we knew.

The river speaks a language, something one isn't born knowing but has to learn. I learned it from my dad. Some of it is wisdom, some of it skill. Some of it is the quirks and tendencies of a natural beast—the ebb and flow, the up and down, the flood draining down to a trickle. It's all part of the river's story, which it's always willing to tell.

Now, I feel that tug to head back into familiar territory, into the backbone of the creeks and sloughs. But then I remember the body, a secret of the shore.

The river can be beautiful, but it can also be ugly.

When I arrive to Bart's, pulling into my usual spot by the shop's fingerprint-smudged glass doors, Lynn's on her smoke break, sitting on a Borden milk crate with a flaming cigarette pinched between two fingers. From a distance, she kind of looks like a praying mantis—wiry arms, bony legs, bulging eyes with a slightly triangular head. She watches me as I slam the truck door. "You ever heard of sunscreen, Clay?"

I lower my cap to my brow and shuffle past.

"Too much time out on that river," she grunts amid an exhale of smoke. "Gonna catch something if you ain't careful."

Coming from a woman sucking on a cancer stick. "And when I do, you'll be the first to know."

I force a tight-lipped smile. Lynn scoffs. What can I say? Tact just isn't our thing at Bart's Bait 'N Tackle. Sarcasm on the other hand? Definitely our thing.

I'm halfway through the door when I hear her voice, echoing back. "Oh, and Clay—Ms. Judy called. And, surprise"—I can almost imagine the curt roll of her eyes, the long drag on her cigarette before she lets the rest of the words go— "she wants some catfish."

"Tell her I quit."

One hand on the door, I turn to face her again, catching the last of Lynn's grin—something both of us know I wasn't supposed to see. "You'd think by now she'd just text your cell."

"Too complicated, and you know it."

Door closing behind, I head over to my side of the store, more accurately known as the bait shop. Hooks, lines, and bobbers are arranged on the far left wall, and shiners—small fish that fishermen use to catch crappie—are stored in a bucket-style container below them.

Lynn works on the convenience side, where customers buy beer, cigarettes, and lottery tickets by the dozen. At lunch, you'll see hot dogs wrapped in tinfoil for the construction workers with short lunch hours, slices of Hunt Brothers pizza in the countertop warming ovens, and Big Gulp cups filled to the brim with Coca-Cola. A couple of times a year, Lynn boils peanuts in an oversized crock pot, selling them in a small paper bag for $3. These money makers—low cost, high profits—make Bart's the perfect river stop.

Bart himself doesn't come around much anymore, drawing his Social Security and preferring to call himself retired. As far as I can tell, he's just an old grouch who stumbles around mumbling curses underneath his breath like a second language. Back in his day, this place served as a Texaco gas station, handed down by his father, but it has taken many forms over the years, changing names more times than I could count. Thankfully, he'd turned the management over to Lynn—she's more of a boss than a coworker—and she makes sure the bait shop and grocery supply profit enough to keep things running.

In the process of stocking one of the barren shelves, I hear the tiny bell thump against the side of the door, the smell of smoke making my nostrils burn. Footsteps patter across the vinyl-tile floor in my direction, but I don't have to look to know who it is.

Lynn's voice crackles, as the words catch on a piece of phlegm on their way out. She might only be pushing forty-five, but she sounds like a seventy-year-old smoker. "Supposed to come a flood tonight. You aren't planning on going back for the day, are ya?"

I rise to a standing position, stuffing my hands in the pockets of my jeans.

No, I want to say. *Of course not.* But that wouldn't be exactly true.

My mind flashes back to Ms. Judy and the catfish I caught earlier; the body, all pale skin and bruises. And I realize that in all of my panic and uncertainty over what I'd seen, what I'd discovered, that I hadn't checked the rest of my hooks.

"Lynn," I say, staring at the floor, the walls—everything but *her*—as my mouth tries to form the words. *I found something out there; something I shouldn't have. And I know it was wrong to leave without calling the police, but I was scared. I was alone.* "How easy would it be to dispose of something in the river without someone noticing?"

Lynn takes a moment to answer. "What's that have to do with a storm?"

I realize how it must sound, but it's the only thing I've been able to think about since locking eyes with the corpse. Besides, Lynn knows as well as I do that most boaters rarely venture out as far as Hidden Creek, which could explain why the swamp isn't already crawling with cops.

Had I been the only one to see it?

"Well," Lynn begins, leaning a leathery arm against the supply cart, "depends on what we're talking about out there. If it's an animal, the buzzards are bound to get to it soon, after the flies, maggots, and gators have their turn with it. And then there's the smell. It'll rot eventually, making it more likely for a boater to find. By then, though, it'll probably be too late." Her green eyes lock with mine, brow furrowing at the same time as her words. I can almost imagine the spinning wheel in her head, and the questions buzzing within the confines of her mind.

"If we're talking about something else"—she pauses, starts again— "I would hope you'd take that up with the police."

If only she knew it wasn't that simple. My record already proves that I've been in trouble with the law, even if it wasn't my fault. Besides, it's not like they'd do anything anyways, and I don't need trouble, cops looking at me for something else I had nothing to do with.

On the other hand, a tiny voice whispers in my ear. *Families need closure, Clay. Wouldn't you like to know what happened if you lost someone?*

I'm reminded of Mom—someone who left when I was too young to understand the aftermath of a failed marriage, lovers becoming strangers, and vows no longer held up to the same merit. For a while, it almost felt like she had died instead of a woman who had left willingly. *I don't know where she is, Clayton. Just let it go,* Dad used to say, when I first had reason to notice the familiar face whose frozen smiles filled the dusty frames throughout the house.

What would it have changed if I knew where she was today? Would things be different if Mom had come back?

Lynn straightens, arms crossed. "I don't expect you're going to tell me why you'd ask something like that? Ya talkin' crazy, Clay."

I lift my cap and run a hand through my brown hair, wishing I knew what to say, how to act, given what I'd seen and hadn't done; given that our conversations had only ever been surface level sarcasm and loaded insults. Will Lynn believe me if I tell her, or will she think it's just some sick joke?

"It's nothing," I laugh, picking up a pack of fluorescent bobbers from the cart and placing it on the top shelf. "I've just been watching a lot of crime shows lately."

Eyebrows raised, Lynn stares back, incredibly pugnacious Lynn who never knows when to keep her opinions to herself. Sometimes, I wonder if it's just part of an act. A brute to everyone else—especially the druggies who crowd the parking lot at night, like moths drawn to a streetlight—but someone I've come to respect for always staying true to herself. "Talking out of your head, kid," she whispers, before rolling her eyes and walking to her station on the other side of the shop.

Still, the thought lingers: *Wouldn't you like to know what happened if you lost someone?*

The words are affirmation enough.

I'll report it, I decide.

Tonight, I'll find the body again to make sure what I saw was real. I'll stare it in the face, snap a photo if I have to, capturing the proof.

Proof that I'm not crazy. Proof that I'm not seeing things.

Tonight, I'll go back.

4

HIDDEN CREEK

A DROP OF RAIN trickles along my cheek as I steer away from the landing, the dark, muddy water a direct mirror of the sky. Engine roaring, wind whistling in my ears, I scan the sides of the bank, mistaking every flash of white for the body, the water dragging her closer to the edge.

Limbs and vines blotting out the sky, I pass beneath a tunnel of trees, just enough room for a boy and his boat to navigate beneath. Gnarled branches reach out for me as I skim past, Spanish moss flails in the wind and partially submerged limbs wave like a ghoulish hand.

In the span of a few seconds, there's a fork of lightning. Then a crash of thunder. A flurry of white egrets swarm overhead, pounding up in a whirlwind of wings.

Something snaps from the left side of the bank, and I reach beneath my seat out of instinct, fingers brushing against the cool metal of the gun. But it's just a branch, slapping the surface several yards away.

Keep going, I tell myself, racing around the bend as the sandbars come into view—one mile down, four to go. Every couple moments, I spot an orange flash in the west, the sun attempting to peek through one final time before dipping below the willow trees. The next two miles are a straightaway, where the massive timbers have succumbed to the erosion of the river, stumps still holding onto the shore, though the tops have slowly begun to lose their battle with the murky undercurrent. Fighting the swift water, I use the tiller to stay in the middle of the channel, watching out for any submerged stumps threatening to trip me up. It's a daily struggle—the river changes every day, and I never know what may lie in my path.

I'm reminded of my first storm on the river—the moment the clouds darkened, the wind shifted, and the animals grew quiet, like they knew; Dad straightening at the rumble of thunder, wrapping the line around his pole and calmly leading us away, out of the mouth of Dead Man's creek, as his shoulders tensed with every flash of light.

Maybe it would've been best to wait until morning, once the threat had passed. Maybe I should've heeded Lynn's warning after all.

The channel splits off to several different sloughs—Walton Creek, Chubb Lake, Gardner Canal—but I keep heading upriver, surrounded by the roar of the wind and the incessant bellowing of bull frogs. A whip-poor-will begins its nightly call, a careful reminder that I don't have long.

Veering off to my right, through a tangle of limbs and palmettos, lies Hidden Creek, a place easy to miss as it is shrouded by overhanging branches.

At last, I'm back in the same place as this morning, but this time I know what I'm looking for. As the creek widens from thirty to forty feet, I stick to the side of the bank, eyes skimming the sand until I hear the telltale sound of strong, flapping wings—a buzzard, vacating its meal. An oily foam drips from its beak; soulless, beady eyes watch as I take in the remains of the woman from earlier this morning. I don't know whether to be relieved or concerned that I didn't, in fact, imagine it.

The denim skirt still hugs her knees, the black bra still clings to her ribs, and her shirt is still torn to shreds, twisted around a nearby limb. All of it suggests the power of a violent river throwing her aside like a mere rag doll onto the bank.

She's closer to the water now. If the current keeps rising from the steady rainfall, there's no doubt that the river will take her in its clutches once again.

This time, I don't get too close, the smell of the corpse and the sight of the maggots crawling between her bones too sharp of a memory to draw any closer. I reach inside my pocket, and raise my phone shoulder level with the shore, zooming in just enough to make out her form. Purple wounds bloom on the woman's milk-white skin. Flies hover in a swarm above. Flash on, I take a few photos before deciding I have enough proof.

Darkness cloaks the swamp now, black as a cave. I fumble for my spotlight in the dry box, pressing a button along the handle as light illuminates my surroundings. Insects flutter around the beam, two glowing red marbles catching the light in my slow retreat.

An alligator. Watching from just above the surface. Then, moments later, the bright diamond eyes of a bullfrog reflect from the distant bank at the same time a sweep of wings glide through the light.

I stretch my phone up to the starless sky, searching for a signal. Hopefully, I'm lucky enough to make the call before I can talk myself out of it. I press the 9, though my finger hovers over the remaining digit.

If the police get involved, then this place might never be the same again. Gawkers, investigators, and all kinds of uniformed men will crowd these banks, disrupting the natural order of life. The whole ecology of the river might even change in the process. More boats mean more traffic, which means more wake, more exhaust, and fewer fish to catch.

I take a deep breath, moments away from making a decision.

Then a voice splits the silence and I almost drop my phone.

"Hey!"

Hands trembling, I cut the engine, willing a glance over my shoulder in the direction of the sound.

"Hands up," the person says again, girlish, high-pitched, and sounding a little unsure.

I pause, all too aware of the gun in the bow, my only defense and protection. But then I notice the outline of a rifle in the beam of my spotlight, the hands lifting the barrel higher, until level with my head.

Blinking, the image sharpens, realization kicking in. I don't know how far I've drifted from the body in my daze, too focused on calling the police versus where I'm going, but I know enough to realize that I'm still in Hidden Creek, near the entrance somewhere, and that a girl in a boat is aiming her weapon on me, a cold glint in her eyes.

"Hands up," she says again, louder this time.

I bite back a curse, managing something between a question and a bargain, voice small compared to the girl's own. "What do you want?"

She studies me, flinching at my question like it's capable of harm. And maybe, it's just enough of a distraction to place the 911 call behind my back.

Her gaze falls to my side. "Drop the phone."

"I will once you drop the gun."

She paces, the water lapping against the side of her skiff, never tearing her gaze away. "I'm going to count to three."

"Are you crazy?" I whisper.

"One."

"You wouldn't."

"Two."

"Listen, we can work this out—"

"Three."

The rifle blast resounds like thunder.

5

SCARLETT

BRACE FOR THE shot, hands flying overhead at the deafening crack, head between my knees. Rain drums on the aluminum boat, trickling along my skin as I grit my teeth and wait for the unbearable pain, the spurt of blood.

One second of silence.

Then two. Then three.

Finally: "You okay?"

Voice so soft I almost mistake it for a friend. Not a girl with a gun and a cold intent to kill.

I blink. *Thunder,* I realize. Not a gunshot, but *thunder.*

Her boat slides to a stop alongside my own, and before I know it, she's offering up a hand. "It's okay. I didn't mean to scare you. I thought you were someone else."

The spotlight brightens her features: blond hair pulled into a ponytail, strands blowing loose in the wind; green eyes racing, inspecting me for harm. Her bottom lip trembles, and I wonder if she realizes her mistake, now that she sees I'm a teenager too.

My gaze focuses on her hand again, nails bitten to the quick, spotless of nail polish or any aspect of color. Who is she? What exactly is she doing here?

My eyes travel down her arms, her legs, which are oddly translucent, skin so pale she gleams like a ghost. She's wearing nothing but a pair of cut-off shorts and an oversized sleeveless white shirt. "What do you want?" I ask again.

"Take my hand."

I wipe the water from my face, squinting through the hazy mist. "What are you doing here?"

Startled by my question, she pulls back. "I could ask you the same thing."

Lightning crackles, electricity humming above our heads, and I duck again, anticipating the flash and crash of the explosion.

When I'm brave enough to open my eyes, she's staring back, unfazed. "My name's Scarlett. What's yours?"

I let go a shaky breath, draw my knees to my chest. "Clayton. But everyone calls me Clay."

"Have you seen the body, Clay?"

My shoulders tense, gaze snagging on the gun behind Scarlett's back, propped against the stern. Forgotten. Abandoned. And, most importantly, out of reach.

"Body?"

"Don't lie to me, Clay."

Rain speckles my face and lashes, though my eyes still manage to meet hers. "Have you been watching me?"

Lips pinching together, she whispers, "Just tell me the truth."

For a moment, we don't speak, nothing but the sound of raindrops pelting aluminum and the occasional rumble in the distance. Scarlett's not going to talk unless I do.

"Look, I don't know what truth you want," I say, not even trying to hide my frustration, "but I was in the middle of checking my hooks when the storm rolled in. Got a little carried away and it was dark by the time

I started to head back. If you hadn't interrupted me by scaring me half to death, maybe I'd be halfway home by now."

Instead of rolling her eyes and acknowledging how much I sound like a dick, Scarlett says, "Really? What did you catch?" She motions to the center of the boat. "Open the live well. Let me see."

A blood vessel pulses in my cheek. "Not until you answer my question."

"And what's that?"

"Why are you out here?"

A smile flickers across her lips. "That's none of your business."

"Is this a game to you?" I ask.

"Maybe. I know you've already lied to my face, so why should I tell you anything?"

"Lied? About what?"

I've barely gotten the words out of my mouth before she speaks again. "You're not out here looking for fish, and I know it." Her gaze falters, if only for a second. "You're looking for the body. A *woman's* body." She cocks her head.

I swallow back a lie. To her, I know how it must look. "You don't understand. I was *scared*. I didn't even know if what I saw was real."

Desperately wishing to change the subject, I gesture off behind her, to the noticeable gap in the trees, something I've never paid attention to in all my years fishing here. "You live back there?"

"Houseboat." Scarlett tosses a glance over her shoulder, as if to make sure it's still there, in all of the shadows of the swamp. "But it's not permanent. Just 'til I can get on my feet."

"You alone?" I ask.

She shifts her gaze down to the water. It's obvious she doesn't want to answer.

"I'm not going to tell anyone, okay?"

Her mouth twitches. "I live by myself, if that's what you're asking. Mama's supposed to be well soon, and then we're out of here."

Where is she now? I'm tempted to ask, but knowing I've likely reached my question limit, I stare in silence.

"It's not safe here," I finally say. "Not with the body."

"I know how to protect myself." A flicker of doubt passes behind her eyes. "But don't tell anyone, okay?"

For a second, I'm not sure if she means about her or about the corpse. Maybe a bit of both. "I don't know."

"Don't." She backs away now, one hand resting on the tiller, the other balling into a fist by her side. "Just stay out of it. I'm fine, and she's already dead."

"Why? She deserves to be found. Wouldn't you like to know what happened if you lost someone?"

"No, Clay. Some people don't want to be found."

I don't like the way she says my name, the tone my mother always used when she was serious. Unlike her, I'm not going to pretend. I don't know anything about her, and based on the way she held that gun to my head, why would I want to?

"I don't need the cops out here, getting in my business, understand?" she says. "I'm doing just fine. Besides, it's likely they'll have a lot of questions. Are you prepared for an interrogation, Clay?"

Stop saying my name, I think. *Stop pretending that just five minutes ago, you weren't holding a gun to my face. Stop acting as if you're concerned about my well-being.*

"Then what do you suggest we do, *Scarlett*?" I ask with a sarcastic tone.

Scarlett yanks a cord on the motor, yelling over the rumble of the engine starting up. "We can talk about this later. See you soon, Clay."

And then, without another word or backward glance, she vanishes into the night.

It isn't long before I'm slipping away through the dark, back toward the landing, toward the safety of home.

In my retreat, my mind circles back to Scarlett. Do I really believe that she's living by herself in Hidden Creek? The place is desolate. And what's the deal with her mother? What did she mean by 'when she's well'?

Part of me thinks her story doesn't add up. Part of me thinks Scarlett's mother left her there and isn't coming back.

Either way, something about her situation doesn't sit right with me. Is it really such a coincidence that a body washes ashore in Hidden Creek around the same time that I discover Scarlett? Why did she hold me at gunpoint? Why is she scared? Who did she think I was?

Why had she been so insistent when I brought up the police? Is it too risky, like Scarlett said? Is keeping the body a secret really worth it? Or is she hiding something?

Trust me, it's not like I want to get involved in a crime. Between Grandpa and Bart's, I have enough on my plate. But maybe Scarlett has a point—maybe she understands what it's like to walk between two worlds, trying so hard to keep them apart. Maybe she thinks if we bring the truth to the police, it will only lead to more trouble. Besides, they're bound to have hundreds of questions. Pair that with the possibility that when the authorities become involved, the river—my place of privacy and escape— might not ever be the same again.

What would Dad do? The question that revolves around my every decision, one that's circled and dug itself into my subconscious.

Trust your gut, Clay, he'd tell me, but trust is a fickle thing. My gut seems to be leading me astray, pointing in all the wrong directions.

My gut tells me: *tomorrow.*

I can't shake the feeling that tomorrow will change everything.

6

PARANOIA

A PALE LIGHT FLICKERS to life above the front door as I crawl to a stop in the drive, almost as if Grandpa remembered to flip the motion detector light on for me.

As I ease the truck door closed and creep up the walk, I can't help but feel as though I'm breaking curfew, even if it's only a few minutes past nine. In a different time, a different life, I can only imagine the reasons I might have for sneaking in after hours: the scent of some girl's perfume on my clothes after a late night or the whiff of alcohol on my breath after some bonfire in the woods. A life where Mom didn't leave and Dad wasn't sick. One where I didn't sneak off to the river every spare moment.

Inside, the house lies in darkness, the pitch-black confirming my suspicion that Grandpa's already asleep. The door clicks shut behind, gentle as a whisper, though I can't help but brace myself for the rush of footsteps in the dark or a light flicking on upon my arrival, as if Grandpa's been waiting up just to ask where the hell I've been. Is it strange to want to be punished just to feel like someone actually cares?

Instead of an angry grandparent, all that waits in the darkness is an empty fridge, offering nothing to cure the pang in my stomach. A silent house, as if its other inhabitants left long before.

I flip a switch, revealing the disarray of the kitchen—dishes piled high in the sink, remnants of pasta clogging the drain, a butter knife smeared with jelly lying on the countertop beside a half-empty can of Dr. Pepper, and a container of moldy donut holes next to the microwave, the glaze appearing yellow in the artificial light.

In the living room, newspapers are scattered across the carpet, local headlines offering glimpses into some of the town's more recent events: *Missing Toddler Found with Companion Dogs, Local Drugstore Chain Files for Bankruptcy.* With the exception of the occasional corpse along the river, this is as exciting as it gets in the one horse town of Delton.

Bundling the papers in my arms, I stack them beside a half-eaten sleeve of saltine crackers on the coffee table next to Grandpa's recliner, crumbs clinging to the vinyl. Usually, a woman from church stops by every afternoon to help keep things nice and tidy, but if I had to guess, all of this accumulated after they left, which makes it my responsibility on top of everything else. Leave it to Grandpa to bring a bit of normalcy to a day that feels far from it.

At the foot of Grandpa's recliner, a dusty picture frame catches my eye. Ignoring the rest of the mess long enough for my curiosity to get the better of me, I lift the frame and stare into the almond-shaped eyes of my mother. I take in her slanted grin, honey-colored hair, and wonder if this would be enough for me to pick her out of a crowd.

Of course, there's always the possibility—one that creeps into my subconscious at night—that maybe she's changed in recent years. Picked herself up, started over again, reinventing the image of a new woman staring back at the lens, hair black or streaked with blond highlights, gaze nowhere near as gentle, but something between sharp and defiant—a woman who's learned from her mistakes.

I wonder if Mom realizes what she left behind. I can't believe I was foolish enough to believe Dad's diagnosis would be enough to make her come back.

Why had Grandpa taken the photo down from its spot on the mantel? What had he seen when looking into this face from the past? Could it have been a product of genuine curiosity or something deeper?

More importantly, how did it end up here, seemingly the focus of Grandpa's chaos?

I trace my steps to the centerpiece of the mantel, swirling my finger through the dust after setting the photo back in its place. A memory surfaces, and I close my eyes, giving in to the moment.

"Clay," my mother whispered, an old Blue Moon crate balanced on her hip. "Look at me."

My gaze hardened, eyes locked on her stark red heels, seconds away from click-clacking down the walk right out of my life. The crate lowered in her arms, tilting, as she bended to my level, a puff of air against my ear. "I'll be back soon."

I didn't even have time to say goodbye before she closed the door in my face.

It's been eleven years since that moment. Eleven years of a mother's absence. A whole decade gone. A promise broken. And what feels like a million possibilities shattered.

Now, all that's left is this photo—one of her young, smiling face. An image that can be interpreted all of its own.

I'd like to believe she loved me, but I'm not so sure how long it lasted.

To me, she is simply a woman who finds the thrill in drifting in and out of other's lives before finally leaving them cold.

That night, I lie awake in the dark, staring up at the ceiling.

The dark is full of sounds, familiar and foreign: the whir of the fan overhead and the popping and groaning of the wooden floorboards out in the hall; a branch, scraping the window glass at every breath of wind; the distant cry of an animal echoing across the stretch of forest in our backyard, haunting and melancholy all the same.

Somehow, the noises remind me of Scarlett, questions buzzing like circuit wires in my mind. Would they remind her of home...wherever home for her happens to be? Or does every splash of a fish and every creak of the houseboat increase her paranoia, making her a little more anxious to stay?

I imagine Scarlett lying in bed, still as a shadow, the covers pulled up to her chin while the barrel of the gun digs against her back. There for protection. *Just in case*, she might say.

Even though I've only met Scarlett once, I can picture the tendrils of blond hair covering half of her face like some exotic zoo animal while she counts in between every beat of silence, one eye open, fingers brushing against the metal of her weapon, in wait.

That seems more like the girl from hours before—one who would shoot if she had to, no matter the cost. One, I assumed, who had experienced something traumatic in her past and felt most confident with a gun in her hands, like the very weight of it gave her power.

Another image begins to take shape, one of Scarlett lying back, staring up at the ceiling like I am now. Whispering secrets in the dark and listening to the sound of them escape her lips, so effortless and natural, lies in preparation for someone like me.

After all, if Scarlett really is alone out there, waiting for her mom to return as she said, she'll need an ally—someone to keep her safe in case whoever left that body decides to leave another.

Scarlett's face morphs into the dead woman's in my mind. Despite her swollen, purple eyes and the nasty wounds gleaming on her porcelain-white skin, something about the woman looked familiar. The dark hair. The denim skirt.

Even though I don't want to entertain the idea, I must have seen her somewhere before. But where?

7

LAST KNOWN LOCATION

As I ROUND the bend to Hidden Creek the next morning, I spot a familiar figure lowered to a crouch in the center of an aluminum Jon boat, tucked away in a corner of tangled Spanish moss and palmettos. After powering off my engine, Scarlett rises to a stand.

"I knew you'd come back," she says. Strands of her dirty blond hair flap behind in the brisk wind, a pair of wrinkled, hand-me-down baggy jeans holding on by a flimsy strip of leather around her waist. Her shirt, the four vampire-pale faces of *The Beatles* emblazoned across the chest, flutters like an oversized nightgown.

"You're a Beatles fan?" I point to the front of her shirt.

"No," she says, looking down at the tops of her worn-out sandals. "Used to belong to my mom."

"Oh."

We stand in silence, with only the sound of rhythmic buzzing of the cicadas in the trees overhead.

"You ready to answer some of my questions?" I ask.

Scarlett eyes me warily. "Maybe. If you ain't a snitch. Promise you can keep all of this a secret?"

I shrug. "Sure. As long as you don't lie to me about why you're here, then I shouldn't have any reason to snitch."

"Alright," Scarlett says. "But I expect the same from you. No lies. No bullshit."

She motions ahead, turning her back to me and snatching a starter cord in the stern. In response, the motor coughs to life in a puff of white smoke. "This way."

I shouldn't want to follow, shouldn't want to get involved in something complicated. I should want to stay upriver, far away from the body and Scarlett, as if our paths had never crossed.

But there are secrets in Scarlett's eyes, something strange and enthralling about her situation, with an opportunity of something more in life than stocking shelves at Bart's and cleaning up after Grandpa drawing me in. It's something more than the mundane, a hint of thrill in obeying the girl whom only yesterday held a gun to my head—the danger and intoxicating excitement that I rarely feel making me give in, like trying liquor for the first time, or getting to second base.

I follow Scarlett down the narrow slough. When she motions right, we squeeze through a small canal just wide enough for our Jon boats. Through a thicket of cypress knees, a glimmering lake emerges, the still water clear as glass.

A gar splashes the surface several yards away, and across the lake, an osprey takes flight, a silver fish clutched in its clawed feet.

If it were any other morning, I might rest in the shade of a tall cypress and lower my cap over my eyes, listening to the distinct hammering of a woodpecker, like a person pounding on a drum, or the noise of beating wings and nearby splashes, reveling in the festive solitude of the river—nature at its finest.

Unfazed by it all, Scarlett continues across the surface of the lake, turning to look back every few moments to make sure I'm still there. On the backside of the wide tributary, hidden in a corner of dense branches and bramble, I spot our destination—a rickety houseboat, accompanied by a wooden dock, the weathered gray siding providing a natural camouflage for the floating square box. A rusty orange top makes it seem to almost blend into the brown leaves of nearby trees.

"Welcome to Lost Lake," Scarlett yells over her shoulder. Five years of fishing along these lakes and creeks and I never once knew this place existed.

She parks alongside the bank, amid a dense clump of sawgrass, hopping out and tugging on a rope clipped to the stern in order to keep the boat ashore.

"Let me help you," I say, sliding to a stop beside her.

"I'm pretty sure *you're* the one who needs help," she answers back, pointing to something floating in the water several yards away.

A long rounded snout of an alligator pokes just above the surface, its green eyes watching my every move. "Don't worry. It won't hurt you," Scarlett says, turning away from the creature and stepping onto the wooden dock. "I call him Big Al. He's been here as long as I have. By now, we're used to each other."

"I still wouldn't get too close," I mumble, as I swing a leg over the side of the boat and follow after, watching the gator out of the corner of my eye all the while. "And don't start feeding the thing or you'll never get it to leave."

Stopping halfway, a small smile flits across her lips. "You think I wasn't smart enough to figure that out on my own? You think because I'm a girl that means I'm stupid?"

The remark reminds me of Lynn, which makes me feel a tad more comfortable around her. If anything, at least Scarlett has a sense of humor.

I glance back toward Big Al, who hasn't moved in the slightest, basking in the early morning sunlight, his eyes seeming to follow us. Hopefully, he'll be gone by the time I have to leave.

Scarlett's hand circles around a rusty knob. Once again, I can't help but wonder if I'm walking into a trap. The door creaks open to reveal a dark room the length of two aisles at Bart's. It's narrow, and smells damp and faintly of mildew and rotting wood. Canned goods stacked from floor to ceiling crowd one corner. Spiderwebs form arches in the doorway and across a couple of the windows.

A dusty, chestnut brown sofa—the springs showing through holes of a probable varmint—occupies one wall, the opposite side filled by a bunk bed. The top bunk overflows with boxes, jam-packed with cans, serving as a makeshift shelf. A kerosene lantern sits in the middle of a faded table, the once amber wood now a honeysuckle yellow.

No TV. No fridge or microwave. No hum of a generator.

Is there even a bathroom? I think to myself.

Scarlett's cheeks redden as I take a small step back in the direction of the door.

"It's not much," she says.

"You live here?"

"Just for a little while. At least until Mama comes back."

"When will that be?"

"Any day now, I'm guessing," she says, but by the hesitation in her voice, I'm not so sure she believes it.

"Do you need food? Water?" My eyes skim over the barren walls and soup cans. "Money?"

Scarlett arches a brow before shaking her head. "No, I got plenty, Clay. I ain't no charity case."

"Seriously. Let me help. It's the least I can do."

She flicks a lock of blond hair out of her eyes, pursing her lips. "I said I'm fine."

The words escape before I can stop them. "Fine. Forget it."

Scarlett doesn't so much as bat an eye. If anything, she feigns a yawn. "I just have to be careful. That's how these things go." She leans in closer. "I don't think you're like that. But Mama would rather me be safe than sorry, in case you *are* like the other guys…"

"What experience do you have with *other guys*?" I ask.

Scarlett lifts her chin and folds her arms as she says, "That's none of your business."

"Did your mom mention where she was going?"

"I don't know. Do your parents always tell you where they're going?" Another strand of hair falls into her eyes, but this time, she doesn't bother with it. "You sure have a lot of questions. You're out here as much as I am."

The words make the skin on the back of my neck tingle. "You've been watching me?"

Scarlett bites back a grin. "Woah. Slow down, Clay. One question at a time."

"I take that as a yes."

Her piercing green eyes scan my face, searching for any sign of danger, any chance that I might not be who I say I am. But I have every reason to do the same. Who knows how many days she's seemingly been stalking me. What's *not* creepy about that?

Still, I know I won't get anywhere without trust. If I want answers, some sort of concrete proof on how her situation and that woman's body connect, then I'll have to start on better ground, have to give something up in the process.

My voice falls to a whisper. "I promise your secrets are safe with me. And I won't tell anyone either, cause I have secrets too."

Scarlett's lips part and her eyes meet mine. Now I must have her attention. "What kind of secrets could a guy like you possibly have?" When I don't answer, she arches an eyebrow. "Okay, I take it you're not going to tell me. I get it…why trust a girl who carries a rifle around everywhere, right?"

"It's not so much that…"

But she waves a hand, cutting me off. What she says next catches me off guard. "Mama got caught up in something bad. That's all I know. She said she'd be back when it's safe." Scarlett leans against the doorway, blocking my path. "There. I said it. Now, what's your little secret?"

Inhaling a quick breath, I let the words go. "I haven't seen my mom in eleven years."

Scarlett's gaze widens. "What do you mean? Is she…?"

"No. Nothing like that. She left when I was six."

"Oh. That sucks."

"How about your dad?" I ask.

"How about yours?" she says.

I run a hand through my hair. We're going in circles.

"Too many secrets for one day," Scarlett mumbles.

"Tomorrow, then," I say. "Tomorrow we tell each other something else?"

Scarlett blows out a sigh. "*Fine.* Whatever it takes for you to get off my back."

"Then it's a deal."

I turn toward the door and then turn back. "How do I know I can trust you?"

Scarlett laughs, the sound making my heart beat a little faster. "Showing you my hideout isn't reason enough? Besides, if I didn't trust you, I can guarantee you'd already be dead."

She looks up, above the doorway, to a .22 rifle hanging on three wooden pegs—the same one from last night.

"You know how to use it?" To be fair, I'd never *seen* a girl shoot a rifle before.

Scarlett crosses her arms over her chest. "Want to find out?"

My mind scrambles for an excuse. "My shift starts soon," I say, even though it doesn't, not for another two hours. "I have to get back."

Scarlett's smile dissipates and she turns to look outside, as if to hide her disappointment. "Oh."

My cheeks flood with heat. Do I really want to leave her? It's not like she has anyone else to talk to...

I shuffle my feet, guilt building in the pit of my stomach. "I'll be back first thing tomorrow morning. Do you like fishing?"

Thankfully, she nods. "Of course I do."

"I know a spot we can go. If you're up for it."

As I step toward the doorway, Scarlett says, "Just don't be embarrassed when I catch a bigger fish than you. Just because you're a guy doesn't mean anything."

"Is that a challenge?"

Scarlett shrugs, a sly smirk crossing her face. "If you're up for one."

Her eyes on my back, I turn to leave. But two steps across the dock, I'm struck with the worst thought: *I don't want to go.*

"See you later, Clay," Scarlett whispers to my back.

"Tomorrow," I call over my shoulder. "Be ready."

Sliding the boat down the short embankment, I notice Scarlett stalling in the doorway. When our eyes meet, she looks away, down to the water. I follow her gaze.

Two cold-blooded slits for eyes watch from the same spot as before. I can't help the smile that spreads across my face at the sight of the creature. "Bye, Big Al," I whisper.

And then I point my boat north and begin the long stretch back.

Back home, after killing a few minutes before my morning shift at Bart's, I stop in front of a map as large as a stovetop, posted on the dining room wall. Faded and tan from age, the map of the Choctawhatchee river system has every known creek, slough, and lake documented by the state of Florida.

Lost Lake. That's the name Scarlett dubbed her hideout.

I trace my finger along the map. Right to left, from Dead River to Mile Lake. Up and down, from Two Sisters Crossing to Hidden Creek, where I found the body.

The paper cuts off a couple inches before my last known location.

There is no Lost Lake or any other tributary of water beyond the creek where the corpse washed ashore. At least, not one that's been recorded.

Which means one of two things: either the printer cut off a portion of the map or the jungle-like foliage of Lost Lake conceals the place from the air.

An uneasy feeling settles over me, racing from my neck to my toes.

Besides Scarlett, I might be the only other person that even knows it exists.

8

SOMETHING SINISTER

THIS MORNING, ON the five-mile drive to the bait shop, it finally clicked: *Bart's.* I'd seen the woman from the river at Bart's.

I can barely remember when I first saw her. At best, the memory is hazy.

"Sir, can you point me in the direction of the motor oil?"

Long strands of hair—brown, streaked blond in places— falling into her red-rimmed eyes. An air of urgency in her step, in the hand trembling by her side; that panicked look in her gaze that seemed to scream, Can you help me?

"Aisle 3," I replied, voice cool and flat.

I wish I'd taken a closer look. I wish I would have thought to ask where she was from, or where she was headed. At the time, it was just another slow day at Bart's, another curious customer running a tight schedule.

At least, that's what I thought. But now I know better. Every little detail matters now.

Thankfully, Bart hasn't cleared the security cameras yet.

And, thankfully, at this moment, Lynn's on her fifth smoke break. At most, I have five minutes. Five minutes to sneak inside the back office where the camera monitors are located and hope I get lucky enough to roll the footage back to the exact time she entered through those doors.

I head in the direction of the family restroom, down a small hallway off to the side of the convenience store. Instead of stopping, I scan the hall for any sign of Lynn and dart to the only other room, door slightly cracked.

My hand closes around the knob, fingers trembling at the cool touch of metal. *Am I really this desperate?* I think to myself.

As the door groans open, too loud for comfort, my gaze flicks back to the hall, pausing to detect any sign of footsteps, even though all I can hear is the racing of my own heart.

Just do it, Clay, I think. *You don't have time to waste.*

And so I do.

A ceiling fan whirs overhead, slicing the air, papers waving atop a wooden computer desk, chipped and faded from the abundance of sunlight slipping in through the cracked blinds.

This is Lynn's office—a place we've all learned to steer clear of, until it's time to sign our time sheets or have a formal meeting when we've done something wrong.

I'm not supposed to be here, which makes my movements faster, my hand enclosing around the mouse out of impulse as I hover over Lynn's worn black office chair. A knot forms in my throat, and all I can hear is the whoosh of blood throbbing in my ears.

I glance at the clock on the screen.

Four minutes left.

The monitor screen displays four panels with different camera angles shaped into a neat square, the time ticking away near the bottom of the grainy surveillance footage. Based on the live feed from Camera #2, Lynn's sitting on a Borden milk crate fifteen feet from the entrance, an ashy haze filling the air around her.

As long as she stays there, I'll be good.

I double-click on a calendar icon off to the side of the tape, selecting the date. The timestamp freezes for a second, each camera image blurring. Then, the images accelerate, rewinding to three days prior, back to Monday—the last time I remember seeing her.

Once the footage halts, a flicker of movement catches my eye in the lower left-hand side of the screen, in the panel of the camera angled directly above the cash register. But it's just Lynn, ringing up a senior customer.

Another viewpoint displays my own fuzzy image, bending down and placing a case of artificial lures onto a bottom shelf.

Then: a car, pulling out of the lot on Camera #4, the only other vehicle besides my truck and Lynn's CJ5 Jeep.

She's not here. Not yet.

Fast-forward five minutes. Ten. Fifteen.

My gut sinks as I lock eyes with the time.

My five minutes are up.

Again, I click on the calendar, checking back with the present.

Lynn's still on her bucket, staring aimlessly into the parking lot, cigarette perched between her two front teeth.

Back to Monday, continuing through the same mundane footage events—Lynn counting money in the register, sweeping the floor around check-out; my own blurry figure stocking shelves and sneaking quick peeks on my phone in-between breaks.

No cars. No customers.

Nothing but me and Lynn.

And then, finally, in the top screen, a gray Chevy Impala speeds into a parking spot. One of the side mirrors missing, wires protruding in its place. A long crack runs the length of the windshield, headlights no longer intact.

A brown-haired woman wearing a black T-shirt and denim skirt steps out of the driver's side—tall, hunched over. Slamming her car door, she tosses a quick glance over her shoulder, crossing the lot in a matter of seconds.

The sight of her makes the hair on the back of my neck stand on end. I can't help but inch closer to the screen, hoping to spot something moving in the shadows of the vehicle. Is there someone else inside the car?

She appears on the next monitor, in the second camera's viewpoint positioned above the entrance, looking back over her shoulder once more before yanking the front door open.

Now that I know the end for her, there's no reason to mistake her paranoia or urgency for anything other than sheer fear. Even then, three days before finding her washed-up body on the banks of the river, her movements suggest something sinister—a woman on the run, trying to escape from something. But what? Who?

All the signs I'd ignored. All the clues she'd given me.

I hadn't even bothered to look twice.

Who are you? I think. *Who are you running from?*

I know what will happen next. Seconds later, she'll find me, interrupting my task of stocking, bothering me with a question.

Now, I suck in a breath as a flurry of movement draws my attention away from the woman and back to the parking lot, to the passenger side of the beaten-up Chevy Impala.

The car door eases open. A head pokes out—

The sound of a bell clanking against the front doors in the present sends me leaping from Lynn's office chair. The chair clatters to the ground, wheels spinning in tandem, as I click back to current time, the Borden milk crate sitting empty in the center of the sidewalk.

Lynn is on the move.

My thoughts racing in a panic, and my stomach rising in the back of my throat, I grip the sides of the desk, watching helplessly as a shadow forms on the underside of the door, the silver knob turning...

Suddenly, a phone rings from somewhere inside the store, the sharp sound echoing out in the hall.

On cue, the lock clicks back into place. The shadow retreats.

Knees buckling, I somehow manage a shaky step forward.

"Hello?" a voice answers, so faint I have to strain to hear. It's Lynn, answering the handheld phone near the register.

Adrenaline courses through my veins, and I bite back my fear long enough to slip out into the hall, sprinting for the family restroom. I don't even bother to close the door behind me.

"Clay?" Lynn calls, but I'm already inside, sliding to the floor with both palms pressed to my eyes. Seconds away from being caught. Seconds away from figuring out who else was inside that car.

The woman wasn't alone. Oh God, this changes everything. Was she with a partner? A friend? Or, even worse, a *child*?

And if she's dead, then where is that person now?

9

RIVER MEN

DON'T HAVE TIME to explain myself.

Once I step out of the restroom, Lynn's waiting for me, hands on her hips, eyes narrowed.

The words spill out before I can stop them. "I'm sorry, I didn't mean—"

But Lynn cuts me off. "Clay?" Her hands fall to her sides, cold expression fading. "That was Ms. Judy again."

Oh.

"Thanks for letting me know," I say, swallowing back some half-baked excuse.

Lynn grabs my arm as I turn away, pulling me closer. "Everything okay?"

I wince at the strong scent of cigarette smoke, drawing in a quick breath of air before Lynn has a chance to notice. "Yeah, of course. Why wouldn't it be?"

She doesn't know, I realize. *She didn't see.*

"For a second, I thought…"

But she doesn't finish, closing her mouth and shaking her head.

For a second, I thought you were inside my office. For a second, I thought you were snooping around behind my back.

Is that what she was going to say? Does she suspect something?

I don't stick around long enough to find out. Instead, I lower my cap, square my shoulders, and hurry past, hoping Lynn doesn't have time to notice my blazing red cheeks or my trembling hands. *The woman wasn't alone. Shit, this isn't good.*

I've hardly taken five steps when her voice stops me. "Want to tell me more about that body?"

My blood chills at the words, heart bucking in my chest. Slowly, I turn back around. "What? What body?"

She doesn't even blink. "Yesterday, you asked me what I'd do about hiding a body along the river. Remember?"

How could I forget? I think.

"You know I was just curious. Hypothetical question, really. That's all there is to it."

If Lynn believes me, she does a bad job of showing it. One eyebrow arched, she motions off behind to my section of the store. "Whatever. Get back to work."

At the house, I survey my fish-skinning post that stands like a sentry outside my back door. A long, rusty nail protrudes at the top, about eye-level, the head filed to a point.

Protecting my hand from the catfish barbs, I jam the nail through the fish's head. Next, using a pair of skinning pliers, I peel the skin from under the head down to the tail in long strips, until a small pile lies at my feet.

On cue, the screen door swings open behind me, the sharp scent of Old Spice cologne growing stronger as careful feet patter down the three wooden porch steps into the backyard. I expect to feel a hand on my shoulder, a voice of assurance in my ear.

Dad. Offering some sort of advice while studying my work.

But once the door bangs shut, I realize with a sinking reality that it's only Grandpa. He stands inches away, wearing that same wild-eyed, stony expression like it's a part of his everyday outfit—a faded blue denim shirt tucked into baggy khaki pants.

"Can't this wait?" he grumbles.

"Just finishing up," I lie, wiping my bloody hands on a dirty dish rag before stuffing it back into my pocket. "Do you mind?"

If there's one thing Grandpa hasn't forgotten, it's how to clean a catfish. And if there's one thing he'll never mind doing, no matter his age or medical condition, it's this. He takes the fish in both hands, sliding it off the rusty nail, and spreads it out on a wooden piece of plywood atop a pair of sawhorses—our own makeshift cutting board. A thick-bladed knife in hand, Grandpa inserts the knife-edge into the pink flesh behind the fish's head, ripping through the backbone in one swift jerk.

Watching him open a slit along the mud cat's belly next, guts and yellow fish roe spilling out, I decide to explain myself. "It's for Ms. Judy," I say, in hopes the name will stir some sort of memory. "Judy Jones. Do you remember her?"

To anyone else, it might seem like I'm insulting my grandpa's intelligence, even though the intent is purposeful, an effort to make him snap out of this endless daze he lives in.

"Judy Jones, Judy Jones," he murmurs to himself. "No, I can't say I—"

A quick shake of the head, that deep red crawling up Grandpa's neck at the realization, color flooding into his cheeks. "Actually...yeah, I remember her."

We both know it's a lie, one to offset the undeniable truth that Grandpa's memory is fading. If it wasn't, he wouldn't have shaken his head at the name and wouldn't have blushed as it spurred thoughts he couldn't explain.

If Grandpa still had his memory, he would have remembered that he'd once been married to her.

My voice disrupts the thick silence. "I'm going by tonight. It's not good to keep putting her off. Bad for business."

Grandpa's eyebrows twitch. If the words bring back any sort of recollection, he doesn't show it. "I want you home before dark," he says. "Clear?"

I open my mouth to protest, but what's the use? In five minutes, he'll forget all mention of a curfew. Better yet, he'll forget I exist. "Clear."

With Grandpa distracted with the fish, I turn my attention back to the house, looking up to the second-floor windows, expecting a figure to be staring down at us through the glass.

Mom. Dad. Their ghosts fill this place, haunting every nook and cranny of a residence that feels less like home and more like a prison cell these days. Four walls reflecting every version of myself, providing glimpses into a past that once radiated so many things: happiness, stability, love.

And, most importantly, hope.

Now that both of my parents are gone, all that remains is an ever-present dread. In the past year since Dad's passing, stagnant conversations and a manic silence have descended on our house like a dark cloud, turning every childhood memory sour, every forced smile from the mantel somewhere between haunted and lonesome. Random memories fill my head now: the way Mom buried herself beneath makeup those mornings before work, until she looked more and more like a stranger; the way she used to tuck me into bed, whispering tales of stowaways on a train, heading north; the forlorn look she got whenever I caught her staring out our front porch window, tendrils of smoke rising from a coffee cup.

Dad, clutching his side after running too fast around the house, his labored breathing spurred by a few tosses of a baseball with me in the yard a few months before his diagnosis. Dad and the terse words he uttered to Mom behind their closed bedroom door.

You can't just leave.

We have a child to raise.

It's not safe.

Every memory unlocks a different version of the parents I thought I knew, the first times I caught them playing off script. After all this time, the curtain's been pulled back, and of one thing I am certain: I don't like what I see.

Snapping back into the present, I notice Grandpa's finished, the fish cut into thin filets at the bottom of a plastic bag. Bag in hand, I head in the direction of my boat, parked outside the garage.

"Where are you going?" Grandpa calls after I'm a few feet away. The words bring me to a halt, my attention diverted back to his wrinkled brow, both of his thick white eyebrows resembling fuzzy caterpillars.

It would be so easy to gather my things, slam the door, and drive away, right out of this life and into the next, just like my mother. No one would even miss me. Not Lynn. Not Grandpa. Maybe not even Ms. Judy.

Before I found the body, and before I met Scarlett, I might've done just that—picked myself up and started over again. But now I have a promise to keep, a secret to share with the one person besides myself. Scarlett—a girl with a past seemingly as cluttered as Grandpa's mind, with mysteries glistening behind her eyes.

Her every word, drawing me in. Every smirk the bait I can't resist. I need more.

"I'm going to the river," I say, even though it's far from the truth. I have no intention of returning there today, especially after last night's events, but it's the only falsehood I can give him, without making him feel even guiltier about not remembering the woman whose last name used to match his own.

Besides, if there's one thing Grandpa can recall more vividly than what he had for breakfast, it's the time he spent on the river as a young boy, running barefoot through the creeks, swinging on a threadbare rope into an old swimming hole, or hunting squirrels in the winter along the bank.

We're a family of river men, after all. Like father, like son.

"The river," Grandpa repeats, flat and monotone, like it's a term he's just now heard for the first time. But there's a mischievous glint in his eyes—the first crack in his façade.

His neurologist often compared Grandpa's mind to the rooms of a house. *Some rooms are full, others have nothing at all.*

Seeing a way inside, one of Grandpa's "doors" partially cracked, I ask, "Did you ever find anything out there when you were a kid? Something you shouldn't have?"

Grandpa blinks. Once, twice, three times, a gurgling sound beginning in the base of his throat, like he's trying to form the words. Then his eyes go dark, his mouth closes, and I know I've lost him. "Be back before dark," he says.

Without another word, he takes three shuffling steps up the back porch and slams the screen door with a resounding thud.

10

MS. JUDY

OUTSIDE MY TRUCK'S tinted windows, Delton appears to be slowing down, storefronts flipping open signs in the windows to closed, and cars and SUVs clearing the near-vacant lots for home. A few businesses line Main Street, commonplace for such a small town as this. A bakery. An antique store. Some crummy little pizza place with windows glossed over in colorful window paint or possibly shoe polish, as if a toddler managed to scamper away from their parents and inflict their art at an opportune moment.

Delton is familiar and quaint, if not a little uninspired. *Dull* would be the word to use when describing its streets lined with quaint Mom and Pop shops; neighborhoods filled with cookie-cutter homes all built around one another, like the developers had suffered from a sudden bout of indolence when toying with the idea of Delton's construction.

As the sky fades to gloaming, hues of orange and yellows dimming with the encroaching black, my thoughts return to

Scarlett, all alone out there in the swamp. Without a TV, phone, or running water, the thought sparks a familiar prick at my heart: guilt. It's not safe for her out there. Not with the gators, the darkness, or the freak river accidents like drowning or getting snake bit. And now that a killer is at large, the river is even more unpredictable.

I have to tell Scarlett what I saw on the bait shop's CCTV footage, before guilt and anxiety gnaw away at me completely. I barely ate anything yesterday, and last night, I couldn't sleep. It feels like I'm trapped in a nightmare, like this isn't real life. A day ago, my biggest concern was whether or not Grandpa took his meds, and now it's what might happen if I continue to keep what I know about the woman a secret. I wish I could go back in time and stop her from getting in that car and driving away. I wish I could have helped her escape whatever she was running from before it caught up with her. Maybe then I wouldn't be in this mess and a woman's life would be spared. Maybe then I could continue on with my simple, mundane life, without all these secrets multiplying inside me like cancer.

Soon, the buildings give way to trees and a house appears out of the wood. Against the growing darkness, its windows glimmer with warm lamplight, and a murky shadow forms behind a windowpane closest to the front door after I've parked in the drive.

Halfway to the front porch, the creak of rusty hinges pierces the silence, and a phlegmy voice calls out, "Clayton Thomas? Is that you?"

"It's me." Hurrying up the porch steps with the bag of fish filets in hand, I take in the woman standing feet away. Ms. Judy, all papery skin and whisper-thin features—narrow lips, sparse eyebrows—scrunches her face into a look bordering on surprise or contempt. "You better have a darn good excuse, boy," she says, reaching forward and pulling me in with a bone-crushing hug.

"I'm sorry," I mumble into her shoulder. "It won't happen again."

"No need for an apology, dear," she laughs, letting me go. "I know how busy you are."

If only you knew, I almost say, but I bite back the words.

"Come on in." Opening the front door, she gives a slight wink. "Let's head inside. We've got some catching up to do."

Even with the sky approaching nightfall and Grandpa's warning flashing through my mind—*be back before dark*—I push the thought away and follow after her. If it were anyone else, maybe I wouldn't feel as obligated to stay. But she's been expecting me, calling off the hook—one of the few people in this town who cares enough to stay updated on my business.

Besides, I feel, in some way, indebted to her. She'd once been family after all, a wife to Grandpa after his first marriage failed and a childhood friend before that. They never had any children together, even if they were married for over twenty years.

Inside, the space smells distinctly of mothballs, laundry detergent, and roasted coffee beans—an odd combination that makes my nostrils burn. The strong odor seems to seep into my skin, my clothes, just like the body's overwhelming scent of decay. Only, this time, I resist the urge to hurl, thinking of Ms. Judy sipping a cup of coffee over the morning paper instead of the lifeless, rotting corpse.

Dull lamplight illuminates a small living room comprised of a green-velvet recliner, a sagging leather sofa, a fingerprint-smudged coffee table, a large rectangular tube television set, and at least half a dozen mousetraps.

Ms. Judy shuffles to the recliner, pointing one long, bony finger in the direction of the shabby couch. "Have a seat, dear, and don't mind the mess."

By *mess*, I assume she means the pack of half-eaten peanut butter crackers lying in a pile of orange crumbs beside the sofa, and the clutter of crossword and Sudoku puzzle books throughout the room—spilling over the baskets arranged in front of the television set, wedged between couch cushions, and propped beneath the clawed feet of the coffee table.

I feign a smile, sitting on the very edge of the sofa, back straight as a pencil. At my arrival, a family of roaches skitter back beneath the couch, abandoning the pack of crackers. My head grows faint.

"Look at this, Clay." Ms. Judy removes a hand-stitched quilt from the back of the recliner, pointing out several small holes in the material, gnawed by the sharp teeth of tiny rodents. "Them dern rats been at it again. Sneaky scoundrels. Don't know if I'll ever catch 'em all."

My smile widens, a betrayal to the revulsion brewing inside, leaving an acrid taste in my mouth. "I hope I'm not keeping you."

"No, no. Enough of my grumbling." Gripping the edge of the lounger, Ms. Judy plops down with a heavy sigh, the tattered quilt now splayed across her lap. "I want to hear about you."

Silence lasts a second too long. "I'm fine," I blurt, hoping she doesn't have a chance to notice the purple bags beneath my eyes or the way I fail to return her gaze. "Just trying to keep busy until school starts back."

"Senior year, right?"

"Right."

Ms. Judy sighs. "The good old days."

The tumultuous part of me wants to hear all about those years. All the dares she took, the lies she told, the parties she crashed. The bonfires she got drunk at while her parents thought she was asleep. The boys she fell for at a time when she was foolish enough to believe that every relationship would last.

But another part of me—the foolish, cynical side—wants to ask if any of it was ever really worth it. If, in the end, it's only four years of our lives we look back on with shame and regret, wondering if our actions only rushed the process, severed ties, and closed more doors than opened.

After all, if there's one thing I've learned from Dad's passing, it's that some of the best moments aren't the ones that come with the most euphoric highs, like dating the prettiest, most popular cheerleader, scoring the winning touchdown, or being accepted into the most prestigious college.

Instead, the best moments are the simple things, like falling asleep to one of Grandpa's fisherman stories, back when he could still remember every vivid detail; sitting in Mom's lap as her finger traced every line of a fairytale; and listening to Dad as he demonstrated how to scope a rifle.

Now, I wish I could explain it all to Ms. Judy, even though I'm not quite sure she would understand. Some of the best moments fall apart whenever they're recounted, overanalyzed, or put into words. After all, how do I explain that the moments spent with Dad in his final days in the hospital were better than any of those in a classroom, listening to some monotone-voiced instructor drone on and on about theorems and chemical components and pretending that I cared, that any of it mattered; better than any Friday night riding around with friends, blasting some overplayed pop song and pretending that none of it would ever get old.

Ms. Judy's voice snaps me from my thoughts. "If you don't mind me asking, how's your grandpa?"

"Fine," I say, before the guilt has a chance to creep in again. "He's doing okay."

"You'll tell him hello for me?"

Like he'll even remember. "Sure." I force a tight-lipped smile. "He'd love to hear from you."

My gaze flits from the floor to the pale-pink walls and back to Ms. Judy, rocking in her recliner with both hands clasped together. I'm not one for small talk—never have been, which is probably why I get along with Lynn as well as I do—but I can feel the question coming, evident in the awkward silence between bouts of light conversation, hiding in our unspoken words.

Finally, Ms. Judy plants both feet on the floor, stopping her relentless rocking to look me dead in the eye. "Clay," she says, just as she always does before suggesting something I'm too polite to ever turn down. *Clay, do you mind swinging by the grocery store for me when you have the chance? Clay, how do you feel about taking my car to the shop for an oil change?*

This time, I know what's coming. "I've been wondering whether you'd mind taking me along with you one of these days."

"You mean, to the river?"

"Yes," she breathes, her silver eyes glinting at the thought. "Haven't been since I was a little girl. But I think it would do these old bones some good, don't you? I know I don't have too much longer. Might as well enjoy it as long as I can."

"Sure." I regret the word the second it leaves my mouth. "I don't mind."

"See what works best for your schedule. I can only imagine how busy you are, hon."

Busy. Like finding a dead body, being held at gunpoint, and working daily shifts all while caring for a senile grandparent is a typical lifestyle for a seventeen-year-old.

Sensing a break in conversation, I stand from the couch and take a step in the direction of the door. "It was real nice catching up, but I'm afraid I've got to head home before Grandpa starts to worry."

Halfway to the front door, Ms. Judy's shrill voice stops me in my tracks. "Son? Be careful out there. Terrible things to happen along that river lately. Hear about that girl? The one whose body they found a couple weeks ago? No one knows who she is. Heard the police can't even find a blood relative."

I poke my head back into the living room, where Ms. Judy's flipping through a *Southern Homes and Gardens* magazine, a pair of outdated spectacles now perched on the tip of her nose. "I can't even imagine what kind of danger that girl got herself into."

"I heard she was a runaway."

Ms. Judy doesn't even blink, holding up a magnifying glass and tracing her finger beneath the lines of the page. "I thought so, too. That is, until I overheard the men talking about it down at the café. Something about her tattoo."

"Tattoo? What kind of tattoo?"

She watches me out of the corner of her eye, a small grin forming on her paper-thin lips now that she has my attention. "Something about a symbol—some pyramid-like thing on her shoulder."

"How is that important?"

"They think she was part of a gang, I suppose. *That* or some cult. They branded her with it, as a way to identify her in case she happened to escape. At least, that's the talk." Looking down, she flips a page of the magazine. A chill settles in my bones at Ms. Judy's next words. "And they don't think she's the only one they'll find."

11

A MILLION QUESTIONS

THE NEXT MORNING, the river has changed its mood, proof of the old timer's story about the tributary inheriting a personality. Angry one day, swift and rising. Friendly a week later, calm and gentle, giving generously of her fish.

Currently, the dark green water is too fast to keep my fishing line in one spot, snaring my bait on every submerged log and fallen limb in my path.

Scarlett, however, appears to have her own issues. Every time she tosses the pole back, attempting to cast her bream buster in an area off the stern of the boat, the nylon line catches in the finger-like branches overhead.

"I thought you said you were good at this," I mumble, attempting to pull the line free for what feels like the hundredth time.

"Keepin' ya on your toes," Scarlett says, standing just behind now, biting back a smirk.

"It's pointless anyway." Tugging on the line only makes it worse—taut and unbending, until it snaps like a rubber band, the bobber slapping the surface and drifting away faster than it takes to blink. I mutter a curse.

The boat trembles slightly as Scarlett steps forward, her breath blowing against my cheek. "Don't worry about it," she says, her hand reaching out and settling on my arm, resting a second too long.

When I meet her gaze, I notice she's gone very, very still. Part of me wants to tug away, tell her it's not a problem.

Instead, I stare into her sea-green eyes, noticing the dimple that forms on the side of her face whenever she smiles a certain way, both cheeks flushed. For the first time, it hits me that I'm not alone out here. A girl with a pretty smile and a past I can't even begin to fathom stands inches away, in the same boat, holding my arm and not letting go. I can't remember the last time I've been alone with a girl anywhere, much less in a place where only the whisper of wind through the cypress trees and the soft gurgle of the water murmurs back.

Something loosens in my chest, a knot uncoiling like yarn, freeing a shaky breath. It's only when I'm brave enough to lean a little closer that she lets go, my hopes drifting with the swift current.

"I'm sorry," she says, turning away but not before I catch a glimpse of her cheeks, rosy either out of embarrassment or nervousness.

"What for?" I gather the rest of my line, back turned as I suck in another unsteady breath. Surely she didn't notice me move closer—surely she couldn't feel the racing of my heart, beating faster with every second she held on.

"Never mind," she replies, staring off the side of the boat, into the murky depths. "I hope I'm not keeping you. That's all." When she turns back to face me, I forget about the pole in my hand or the fact that my shift starts in an hour. For once, it's like nothing else matters but finding out the truth about who she is.

"You don't have to keep doing this," Scarlett says.

Noticing my startled expression, she continues: "Coming back here. For me. I'm sure you have other friends you'd like to see. A family at home. People who care."

"I don't mind," I say, the alternative to admitting I have no one else to depend on, except for the few people who play almost nonexistent, temporary roles in my life, like extras in the background of a movie. It's better than giving up that hidden part of myself, speaking the truth out loud—one that can't be taken back.

"I had people back home," she whispers, so faint I have to strain to hear. "But now, none of them matter. Truth is, I doubt they even miss me. I doubt they even care."

"Of course they care. Why wouldn't they?"

Scarlett straightens a little, a grin pushing through her solemn expression. "What's that supposed to mean?"

"Well, you're different for one. In a good way. Not like all those other girls with the fancy clothes and cars and Daddy's trust fund money...the girls whose heads are so far up their asses they can't even see straight. Come on, you know the ones."

"Sounds like you have experience," she says, eyebrows raised. "So, you got a girlfriend, Clay?"

Setting my pole beside me, I tuck my knees to my chest and try to think of an answer. A couple of conversations at Bart's that led to dates with Spring Break girls who'd never bothered to learn my name probably don't qualify. Nothing more than a summer fling.

I'd never been in a relationship like Scarlett might think. And I know that as long as I stay here, in this sleepy town of low opportunity and boredom, that I might not ever experience something like that.

"No," I tell Scarlett. "What about you? Dating anyone?"

Scarlett shakes her head. "Never had time for that. I moved too much."

"Why? If you don't mind me asking."

"Because of Mama's job. We never stayed in one place for long."

"What does she do?"

Scarlett squeezes her eyes shut, leaning back with a sigh. "She was a bartender for the longest time. Then a motel clerk. Then a waitress at some crummy little diner whose name I can't even remember."

"And you? What did you do?"

One of Scarlett's eyes crack open, as if the question catches her off guard. "Well, back when we lived in Tucson, I helped clean motel rooms for money. After that, I washed dishes in a seafood joint in Panama City. Far too much work for minimum wage, if you ask me."

"I work in an old tackle shop called Bart's. Most times, it's slower than catching a fish, but I put up with it. At least I know what I'm working with." I shift uneasily, forcing out the next words. "Speaking of Bart's, I watched the CCTV footage, and it turns out the same woman I found on the bank visited the bait shop a few days before I came across her body. But that's not all: someone was in the car with her, Scarlett. She wasn't alone."

Scarlett sucks in a breath. "Shit. Did you see who was with her?"

"No."

"Shit," Scarlett says again.

"Look, I need to go to the police. What if that person was the woman's friend or child? They need to be found, before whoever killed her gets to them too."

If they haven't already, I think.

Scarlett's green eyes flash. "No," she says. "I understand you want to help, but this is dangerous. You don't need to tell the police anything right now. At least wait a while."

"*Wait a while?* We can't! Another person's life is on the line here. What do we possibly have to lose by telling them?"

With a shrug, Scarlett says, "The police might already know about it. I think you should wait."

"That's not good enough." I exhale and rub my forehead. "If I wait any longer, I'm going to go insane. It's not fair to that woman or the other person if I continue to keep my mouth shut."

"I can't talk you out of it," Scarlett says. "Do what you want. But if you're asking me, I don't think you should breathe a word of this. There are too many risks in telling the police. In my experience, it's best to just stay out of it."

"In your experience? What's that supposed to mean?"

Her words aren't making any sense, only leaving me with more questions, a million of them it seems—ones I'm desperate to know the answer to. They aren't what I was expecting her to say; her *don't get involved* attitude definitely does not make me feel any better. If anything, guilt claws at me even worse.

Scarlett's gaze goes cold, her mouth falling agape for a second, before the moment passes and she looks away. I want to ask her what she is hiding, want to press her with more questions, but I know it'll do more harm than good. When she wants me to know, she'll tell me.

Above, the early morning sunlight creeps through the branches, making the water shimmer with flecks of white, shapes and shadows appearing beneath the surface every now and then.

I sigh, lowering my cap farther down over my eyes. It's time to talk about something else. "I still remember the first time my dad took me here. It's a place you can't describe to anyone, not if you want them to believe it. Have to experience it yourself."

"Why doesn't he ever come with you?"

The reality of that question not one I'm ready to hear myself say out loud, I settle with a lie. Besides, I'm sure Scarlett has her fair share of them. "He's too busy."

"Oh, yeah? How so?"

"He's a bartender." It's the first thing that comes to mind. "Just like your mom."

And then, as if to offset my lie, I offer up a little bit of truth. "My mom didn't stay around long after I was born. So it's always just been the two of us. Well, and my grandpa."

I'm not sure why I feel like Scarlett's earned the right to know this part of my life when no one's ever bothered to ask.

"I can tell you love him," she whispers, after a moment.

The back of my eyes sting, but I blink the pain away. "I do. I really do."

"It's just like Mama. She never left me, not even when times were bad and I only held her back."

"Where is she now?"

Scarlett doesn't answer for a while, as if she's trying to sort out a lie in that head of hers, figure out which pieces fit. "That's the thing. I don't know, Clay. I really don't. She's never been gone this long."

"We'll find her," I say, even though some part of me knows that, deep down, she's not coming back. Maybe it's built out of my own memory—one of Mom click-clacking down the walk in those annoying red heels and driving away without as much as a goodbye. The fact that she could carry me around for all that time and then decide I wasn't worth it.

"I miss her," she says. "I really do. And it doesn't make sense why she would just leave me out here when she's never left before."

"Could she be in trouble? Maybe she needs help."

"You don't think—"

Scarlett lets the words trail away, as if on the brink of a sudden revelation, one that maybe wouldn't sound the best if voiced aloud.

"Don't worry about it. She'll be back before you know it."

But Scarlett just shakes her head, staring aimlessly down at the water, not saying anything for the longest time. When she does speak again, her voice is smaller, devoid of any emotion. "Don't you have to head back soon? I wouldn't want to keep you."

The words are like a sucker punch. *Bart's. 9 o'clock.*

I don't want to leave. For one of the first times in my life, I'm perfectly content with staying right here, with a girl who I feel somehow understands me better than anyone else, even if I don't understand anything about her situation.

"Yeah," I say. "I do."

"Alright, but don't leave me waiting too long."

The smile pushes through before I can stop it, some stupid, sloppy grin that I can almost bet gives away far more than I mean for it to. "I would never."

"And Clay?" she asks, before I can start the engine or grab hold of the tiller, itching to head back; before the noise drowns everything else out. Scarlett—always one for the final word. "Can I tell you something?"

"Anything."

A moment of silence, stretching on longer than it should, until finally: "You're a terrible liar."

"Thanks," I say, rolling my eyes at Scarlett's brutal honesty.

"My pleasure." Leaning back, face pointed to the sky with both eyes shut, a gentle smile forms on Scarlett's lips. "Let's get outta here, Clay."

Once I've dropped Scarlett off and am making my way back to the landing, I slow my skiff at the entrance of Hidden Creek, staring at the edge of the bank. As my eyes comb over the sandy-white shore, Scarlett's words come back to me: *Just stay out of it. Some people don't want to be found.*

The woman is gone. Just as I suspected, she's been swallowed up by the river, lost to the current, the only proof she was ever here a black T-shirt twisted around a nearby limb. Well, and those photos I took with my phone.

My gut clenches, so tight it's hard to breathe. My stomach roils, and I know it's not because I'm hungry. It was my responsibility to make sure she was properly interred and her family was notified. But I let Scarlett talk me out of it, and now it might be too late.

I won't let her talk me out of it any longer.

I know what I need to do.

12

FACE OF A FUGITIVE

ATER THAT MORNING, on the last pay phone in Delton, I make the call. Anonymously, I tell the 911 operator that a fisherman saw a body floating in the river near the landing. I make sure not to mention any landmark remotely close to Scarlett, just to keep the police out of her business. The moment I hang up, I feel fifty pounds lighter.

I should've made the call two days ago, but it's done now; the police will be looking for her, and hopefully the woman will receive the proper burial she deserves.

Soon after, with not a second to spare, I arrive at Bart's Bait 'N Tackle. This morning, a maddening silence fills the shop. For once, there are none of Lynn's mumbled curses whenever she happens to notice me on my phone or any of her comments about the latest front page story in *The River Gazette*. In fact, there is no sign of Lynn at all.

Outside the storefront windows in desperate need of cleaning, the small lot sits empty, near vacant, except for my F-150 truck in its usual spot by the front door. Unfortunately, the lack of business doesn't mean I don't have a thousand other things to do around here.

In fact, Lynn left a list of chores on the front counter. But instead of sweeping the floors or stocking shelves, I head toward the back of the store in the direction of Lynn's office.

On the way, my fingers brush against something in the bottom of my jeans pocket—a flash drive. Something I snatched from home after receiving Lynn's text about a doctor's appointment out of town.

Now with the whole place to myself, I don't have to worry about Lynn catching me. A couple of minutes later, hunched over her computer with the drive inserted into its rightful slot, I roll the footage from Monday, when the Chevy Impala came to a halt in a far corner of the lot.

My hands shake with excitement, my chest a bundle of nerves. I'm about to find out who else was in that car, perhaps the last person to see this woman alive.

Onscreen, the passenger side door opens, a head poking out, just as a bell clanking against the front door snaps me back to the present.

Footage still rolling, I back away from the computer and trace my steps to the entrance. A man stands just inside. White button-up shirt. Dark dress pants. Brown leather boots, with both hands tucked inside his pockets. He smells faintly of cigarette smoke.

"Can I help you?" I try to sound calm, but my voice comes out shaky, breathless.

The man takes a step closer. "Are you Clayton Thomas?"

"I am. What can I help you with?"

Grandpa. The thought makes everything else slow, the room beginning to spin. "Is something wrong?"

He removes an object from his pocket, turning it over and holding it in front of my face. It's a gold badge.

"I'm Detective Conaughey with the Sheriff's Department. Mind if I ask you a few questions?"

Detective. Sheriff's Department. The only words I catch. Ones that lodge themselves inside my brain like shards of glass. This can't be about Grandpa. But if it's not, then why is he here?

Lynn, I tell myself. *It has to be because of Lynn.*

A domestic dispute with her boyfriend. Or, even worse, a car accident. Maybe Lynn was caught with drugs?

"Don't worry, son. You're not in trouble." Detective Conaughey places the badge carefully back in his pocket. "I just want to know if you've seen any shady-looking characters around here lately. Particularly a woman and her daughter. The daughter should be around your age."

At his words, images from the security cameras play like a movie reel in my mind: the beat-up Chevy Impala coming to a stop, a woman stepping out and glancing behind herself once. Two times.

My mouth is so parched that the word almost gets stuck there on its way out. "No."

The detective sighs, fingers trailing through his stubby black beard. His eyes are bloodshot, dark bags bulging beneath them, and it makes me wonder how long he's been up. "According to other witnesses, they were passing through this area. I have reason to believe they might be hiding out somewhere, possibly along the river." His eyebrows rise. "I'm guessing that's your boat in the parking lot? If so, I take it you know your way around out there pretty well."

My heartbeat spikes, what was once a steady throb now an accelerated rhythm. "I know it."

He reaches inside his pocket again, retrieving a piece of folded paper. When he holds it out to me, I have no choice but to take it.

"That's the girl's photo. Maybe you've seen her somewhere along the river? If you have, it'd really help if you let me know."

Smoothing out all the lines and creases, I stare down into the face of a fugitive, according to the word *Wanted* bolded across the top of what appears to be a DMV photo. The girl has blond, almost yellow hair. Green eyes. A smattering of freckles across the bridge of her nose.

DOB: 10/17/2004

Name: Danielle Brown

But even with the clear difference in names, it's undeniable who this is—a girl who has been lying to me this entire time.

A girl who said her Mom was coming back soon, like it was some sort of casual vacation. A girl who held a gun to my head like it wasn't her first time. *What are you up to Scarlett?* I think.

"No sir. I haven't seen her."

If the detective notices my flaming red cheeks, how I fail to meet his gaze, or the way my fingers tremble as I hand back over the paper, he doesn't say anything.

But Scarlett's voice still edges into my mind: *You're a terrible liar.*

"Well, if you see her, please don't hesitate to call this number," he says, placing a business card on the front counter. One hand on the knob, door halfway open, Detective Conaughey turns back to me before letting it close. "And if you do see this girl, don't approach her, alright?"

Too late. "What did she do?"

The man's gaze falls to my feet. A beat of silence, as if he's deciding whether to tell me or not. Finally, he looks back up, takes a deep breath, and lets the words go. "She's wanted for the death of her father."

13

BETRAYAL

AFTER **DETECTIVE CONAUGHEY** leaves, I spend the remainder of my shift in a daze, absentmindedly completing the chores Lynn left while staying far away from her office in the process. Some part of me knows who will step out of that car, and another part doubts whether that girl the detective warned me about—someone I've been returning to day after day—is the same person.

Still, by the end of the shift, I can barely wait to get home to power on my computer, insert the drive with the downloaded footage, and find out once and for all. No more guessing. No more wondering.

Only the truth.

Later that day, in the confines of my room, I hold my breath as I type in my username and passcode, dreading and anticipating the answer all the same.

It's *her*. Even before replaying the footage, I know. All the pieces fall into place in my mind.

Onscreen, the car door opens. A head pokes out.

Blond hair, just like the woman's. Pale, almost translucent skin gleaming in the harsh sunlight.

Scarlett (or is it Danielle?).

The realization of it all makes a tight knot form in my chest. It seems to wrap around my organs, squeezing and constricting them with every breath.

She lied to me. Quite possibly about everything.

Her name, her past, and her mother, whose body I'd found washed alongside the river less than three days ago.

She's wanted for the death of her father, Detective Conaughey said.

The back of my eyes burn when I close them, stinging with sweat and salt and betrayal.

How was I to know she was a killer, or that everything she'd told me was all part of a carefully constructed lie?

My fingers travel across the keyboard in search of more answers. According to Google, there are thousands of Danielle Browns in the U.S. Endless Facebook profiles. Dozens of YouTube channels. Filtered photos made up of girls of varying ages.

This is how many Danielle Browns exist, and yet, I'm still not exactly sure if that's Scarlett's real name or one she borrowed from someone else.

No search leads to any sort of concrete proof. No Danielle Brown wanted for the death of her father. No Danielle Brown currently on the run, her smiling face marked *Missing*.

It's almost as if the girl hiding out along the river doesn't exist. As if she's only ever been a stranger—someone I was foolish enough to believe I could trust.

I don't know what to expect later that afternoon as I round the bend to Lost Lake, coming to a stop in a clump of palmettos on the sandy bank. But Scarlett is waiting for me, pushing open the front door and stepping out onto the dock.

Her smile immediately fades when her eyes catch mine.

"Clay? What's wrong?"

"You need to stop lying to me, Scarlett." I push myself to my feet, fists balled by my sides, but I don't step out of the boat. If she's anything like the girl Detective Conaughey warned me about, I don't have any intention of getting closer. "Or is that even your name?"

"Don't do this," she says. "*Please. I can explain.*"

"Go ahead. Explain everything, *Danielle*."

Scarlett's green eyes widen. "Who are you?" she asks, with a careful step in the direction of the door.

"I could ask you the same thing."

"Who are you?" she asks again, louder this time.

"All I want is the truth. No bullshit...okay?"

But Scarlett isn't listening. "Did you talk to the police? Is that how you know?"

Adrenaline courses through my veins. "They told me what you did. Said to stay far away...that you were dangerous."

"They don't know anything." She shakes her head. "And neither do you."

"I know that you're on the run. That your mother isn't coming back."

Scarlett hesitates a second too long, enough for me to realize that my words are truth. "And why is that? Why isn't she coming back?"

"Because I found her," I say, not even bothering to hold the secret in any longer. "The body...that was your mother, wasn't it?"

Scarlett's shoulders slump, and instead of answering, she collapses onto the creaking wooden floorboards, palms pressed to both cheeks. "I shouldn't have stayed here," she mumbles, over and over again. "I should have left the second I knew she wasn't coming back."

"So you've known your mother was dead!"

"*He* did this," she says, more to herself than to me. "*He* killed her..."

"Who? Your father? Is that why you murdered him?"

"Seriously, Clay?" She lifts her face from her hands and glares back at me, bottom lip trembling. "For Christ's sake, you honestly think I'm a murderer? Well, I hate to disappoint you, but I'm not. Just like my name isn't Danielle."

I take the first step out of the boat, feet meeting solid ground, before crossing the dock and bridging the gap between us. I told myself I wouldn't do this. The plan was to stay inside the boat, away from *her*.

Either she's genuinely upset or one heck of an actress, but I find myself believing her and I don't even know half of the story. There's no way the same girl who had my heart racing at the slightest touch only the day before is capable of murder.

But the memory of that gun in her hands makes me skeptical.

Hands up, she'd said, with the rifle pointed at my head. Warning me, but at the same time giving me a chance. Is that really something a killer would do?

Now, it seems more like a desperate cry for help, a warning formed out the fear of knowing what had happened to her mother and knowing it could happen to her too.

I recall the feeling of someone close by that morning as I discovered the corpse. Scarlett. The whole time, it was Scarlett. "You *watched* me find her," I say. "But if you knew what happened, how could you leave your own mother?"

"Because I was scared!" she says. "I didn't know what to do! Don't you think I hated leaving her out there alone? Besides, I was hoping someone would find her after a while, so I wouldn't have to touch her."

My hands grip Scarlett's shoulder, squeezes. "Look, I'm sorry and I know it's hard, but I need you to tell me the truth. Everything…I need you to tell me everything, Scarlett. I can't help you if you keep this to yourself."

She speaks into her hands, and I have to strain to hear what she says next. "How'd you find out who I was?"

Was, not *am.* As if she used to be someone else. A girl with a different name and a different life. One who hid in the kitchen of some diner in Panama City, scrubbing dishes until her fingers went numb, if anything about her past is to be believed. She owes me nothing and everything at the same time.

"Listen, you can't tell the police any of this," she says, before I can answer. "Not about me or Mama. It's not safe."

"A cop came by the store yesterday where I work. Showed me one of your pictures and told me to keep an eye out. He thought I'd be able to point him in your direction." I expect this to be the moment where she snaps or breaks down in a fit of hysterics. The fact that the police are asking around and even bothered to reach out to me in the first place suggests the authorities are one step closer to locating her hideout.

Instead, Scarlett's gaze flicks to her shoulder, where my hand still lingers.

When I drop it, she asks, "What did this cop say he wanted me for?"

She scowls at me, but I keep my face blank. "He said you were wanted for the death of your father."

"Bull," she grits. "As far as I know, the bastard's still alive."

"Why would the cop lie?"

She shrugs. "I have no idea."

"So what are you doing out here? And why is your mother—?"

"Someone found out about us," she says, before I can finish that sentence. "Someone who didn't like what we were doing."

"What do you mean?"

"Not here, Clay. *Please*, not here. It's not safe."

"Then where do you want us to go?"

"Dead River," she says, standing up and motioning toward my boat. "Come on. If you want the truth, then let me show you."

14

DEAD RIVER

SCARLETT GIVES DIRECTIONS while I navigate, pointing down narrow creeks and channels, all the while keeping her voice so low and faint I have to strain to catch her words over the rumble of the motor. I'm still not exactly sure where we're headed or if I can even trust her enough to know she's not leading me into some sort of trap.

First a body, and now a girl stranger than any I've ever met—a possible fugitive, leading me to a place I've only heard referenced in legends.

Dead River—the center of some story Grandpa used to tell around the campfire, back when I was foolish enough to believe anything.

A tale of a whirlpool, snatching a man under while fishing in the middle of the current, snagging him on a root or treetop, never to be found again. It was the first time I knew the river to be murderous.

As we grow closer, the landscape of clay and muddy water fades to a sandy-white shoreline and waters the color of black coffee, due to the influence of tannic acid from the leaves.

Spanish moss hangs from nearly every branch, casting long, thick shadows across the sand.

The breeze calms to a mere breath of wind, the only movement some water bugs that resemble spiders, darting across the river's surface. Gone are the splashes of the gar, and the occasional squawk of water fowl.

True to its name, the place is sinister. Dead.

At the water's edge, a line of quaint wooden structures appear. Most of them seem to slouch, most likely from past hurricanes and rainstorms, hovering on stilts like old men trying to balance themselves with a cane. The wood toward the bottom of the frames are pock-marked and water-stained, with wounds of previous floods and debris striking the planks.

"Mama used to come here all the time," Scarlett says once I power off the engine, her voice cutting through the eerie silence of the swamp. "When she was a girl, she learned to fish along the bank and dry her clothes in one of those shacks. That's probably why she felt so comfortable leaving me out here. Thought I could fend for myself. She'd experienced the survival of life on the river and thought I could too. It's in my blood, I guess. We're just that type of people."

With one look at the abandoned fishing camp, it makes me wonder if anyone's stepped foot in this place within the past decade, much less the past year. Something about the sight of an old clothesline strung between two porch posts on the shore makes a pit form in my stomach. Maybe it's the stigma of Grandpa's tale, still fresh in my mind after so many years, or maybe it's the feeling that we're not the only ones here.

"You had something you wanted to show me?" I ask.

Scarlett clenches her jaw. "Stay quiet," she says.

Scarlett leads while I follow, my long, lanky legs struggling to keep up. After several steps, she casts a quick glance over her shoulder, in the direction of the Jon boat parked in a cluster of cypress knees.

"Is someone following us?" My voice echoes louder than expected here, among the seclusion of the forgotten fishing camp.

Scarlett raises a finger to her lips. "Not a word," she mouths.

The only other sound the trod of our footsteps across boggy sand, sloshing and scrunching with every step, we pass shack after dilapidated shack, avoiding busted beer bottles and sparkling glass shards catching the morning light. My gaze skims over the rest of the shore, before snagging on some faded political sign tossed in the dirt at the base of a decrepit porch, spray-painted over with the words: *No fussing, no cussing, no cigarette butts.*

I'm just about to ask what we're doing here when Scarlett stops, holding out a hand.

"You hear that?" she whispers.

For several seconds, all I can discern is the racing of my own heart, thundering in my ears from trying to match Scarlett's pace. Then the sky begins to hum, faintly at first, before I detect the whirr of a distant engine high above our heads. It only grows clearer, louder, with every second we stand still, holding our breath at the sound.

"Inside. Now!"

Before I can protest, Scarlett's grabbing my hand, pulling me after her.

We race for the last shack at the far end of the bank, the far echo above now a steady roar. Beneath our feet, the ground tremors slightly, pulsing with every thrum of the copter's rotors.

A second later, Scarlett's free hand encloses around the door's rusty knob, and then we're inside, gasping for breath.

The smell hits me first—some damp, musty odor akin to mildew. Scarlett closes the door and peeks out a window, while I stand in the center of the room, clenching and unclenching my fists.

"What's going on?"

"Not now, Clay."

The room feels like a sauna—compact and stifling. "It's only a helicopter. What's your problem?"

"Do you want them to find us?" she hisses, never once tearing her gaze from the window.

The room vibrates, the noise even closer now, reverberating so loud across the swamp that I feel it in my teeth. I count the seconds, waiting for the copter to pass. But it lingers, possibly at the edge of the tree line now, as if in search for something. Or some*one*.

I stick both hands into my pockets, fumbling around for anything useful.

A gum wrapper. A couple of loose coins. Detective Conaughey's business card.

Nothing I can use to protect myself because what I need most I don't have.

A gun, beneath the seat in the boat parked several hundred yards away. Retrieving it might pose a risk, if whoever's in control of that helicopter is, in fact, after us.

Or maybe Scarlett's reason for coming here stems from a fugitive covering her tracks, on the run from the law. Using me as her aid, her back-up plan. Someone to get her place to place without raising suspicion.

But she should know now that I'm done playing by her rules.

We stand in silence for what feels like forever, listening to the drone of the helicopter as it fades farther and farther away. It's not until it's gone completely that Scarlett turns back in my direction, cheeks drained of color, gaze glassy and unfocused.

"They could be anywhere, Clay."

"Who?"

But Scarlett doesn't answer, brushing past me and squatting to the floor a couple feet away. With her back to me, concentrated on something else, I have plenty of time to make a run for it.

I take a step back. Two steps. Three.

I'm at the door, knob in my grip, as Scarlett reaches a hand down beneath a noticeable gap in the wooden floorboards and lifts something out into the light.

It's a journal—one with a forest-green cover and pages the color of dust.

Seeming to forget my previous plan, my hand falls away from the knob and I take a step closer. "What's that?"

Much to my surprise, Scarlett doesn't answer, instead flipping through the book until coming to a stop on one of the final pages. She holds it out to me, still refusing to look me in the eye.

Taking the journal in both hands, I notice the red and black ink scrawled across the white page. A messy scribble of letters. Two words for nearly every line.

They're all names.

Sarah Hayes.

Anna Miller.

Haleigh Thomas.

Toward the bottom, the names become more difficult to pronounce.

Anastasia Abramova.

Olga Palahniuk.

Svetlana Kuznetsova.

"Who are these people?" I ask.

Scarlett doesn't even blink. "Prisoners," she says.

15

A BAD IDEA

"**WHAT KIND OF** prisoners?"

"All kinds. Most of them are sold into drug rings or prostitution." For the first time since our arrival, she pauses long enough to look me in the eye. "Mama used to be in one of the rings when she was much younger. But she escaped it, told me someone smuggled her to the river. I don't know who."

The pit in my stomach grows. "I don't understand. If this happened a long time ago, why was she still in danger?"

Scarlett draws a long breath, as if in preparation for the truth. I can't help but wonder if I'm the first person she's ever told. "She got involved with it again much later, but in a different way. She got a job running a bar, knowing she could hire some of the trafficked girls to work for her. It was a way for the girls to trust her so she could pick one out to help."

I swallow back the lump in my throat. "Oh my God. Did

one of the men from the ring suspect she was helping the girls? Is that who's after you now?"

Scarlett doesn't answer. Instead, she gestures for me to pass over the book, but I hesitate, staring down at the list of names.

Twelve women. Some Scarlett's age, according to the book. Some even younger.

Suddenly, I feel like I'm going to be sick.

Scarlett takes a shaky step forward, one hand coming to a stop on top of the scribbled page, the other gripping my shoulder. "If something ever happens to me, give this to the police, okay? Until then, there's something I need to do."

But her words fail to sink in. "Did you write all this? Are these some of the women your mom was trying to help?"

Her grip on my shoulder tightens, the whisper in my ear more desperate than before. "It's time to go, Clay. We can't stay here for too long."

The book slides out of my grasp. I don't even try to stop her. I never want to look at that book with its tattered forest-green cover and foreign names scribbled inside ever again.

With the journal back in its previous spot, beneath the faded, dusty floorboards, Scarlett heads for the door, stopping to cast one last look out a passing window before stepping outside.

"Come on, Clay," she says. And then she's gone.

Everything within me wants to call out for her to stop, to tell me more.

But I know I should be thankful that she's given up at least one secret—one I have to admit I was in no way prepared for.

So, without as much as a second thought, I swing the door closed and follow after.

Back in the boat, a hundred different questions come to mind. How many people were involved in keeping twelve women quiet long enough to profit off of them? Where did they all stay?

And, most importantly, why hadn't anyone ever bothered to turn in a kidnapper after so many years?

A few minutes later, in a straightaway between Lost Lake and Dead River, I kill the engine, watching Scarlett's expression morph from a numb sort of calm to one of alarm.

"What are you doing?" she asks, lowering to a crouch with one hand gripping the boat's gunwale.

"I have more questions." Scarlett may have given me the truth, but there are too many other pieces waiting to be snapped in place.

Scarlett's face drains of color. "Can't this wait?"

"I'm tired of waiting. I need to know."

"This is a really bad time."

"Who's after you?" I blurt. "Can you tell me their name?"

No response. Just the steady rise and fall of the current, the whisper of the wind.

It's time to try another tactic. "Please, Scarlett. After everything I've done for you these past several days, you could at least give me a name."

Scarlett's hands ball into white-knuckled fists. "Fine," she says through clenched teeth. "But then we're out of here, alright?"

A beat of silence. "I never knew any of their names. But there was one man she talked about a lot. She met him at the bar where she worked and they fell in love. Of course, for the longest time, she didn't know that he was also involved in the same ring she was trying to help those girls escape from. He was the ringleader in fact, and once Mama found that out, she got the hell out."

"Is this the same person who's after you now?"

Another pause. Another sigh. *Just spit it out already,* I want to scream.

"I'm not for certain, but I think so. All I know for sure is that Mama helped smuggle a lot of the trafficked girls out of the cities, since she used to be a slave herself and knew how difficult it was to escape. She did this for years without anyone finding out. Until now."

"How did they catch on to what she was doing? Did she involve you in this?"

Yards away, something purrs from the riverbank, but I shift my eyes to the sky, expecting a helicopter to skim past the treetops at any given second.

Still, this sound is closer, and far too muted for any kind of aircraft.

My gaze sweeps across the opposite bank from the center of the straightaway, in search of an idling boat or a fisherman, waving a hand and staring a second too long.

But there's nothing.

Scarlett opens her mouth, closes it, then opens it again. "We really need to go," she finally says.

"You still haven't answered my question," I repeat.

Just as she starts to speak, the truth possibly moments away from spilling out, a deafening crack from somewhere behind us breaks the silence. In an instant, something collides with the water, droplets splashing our faces.

Another ear-splitting crack. Another splash.

Adrenaline zips to my toes as I realize.

It's bullets.

16

BLACK SPOTS

AN ECHO RESOUNDS across the water. For a moment, time seems to stand still, a flock of speckled-gray herons from the shore hovering in mid-air, while both of us freeze.

Then everything goes to hell.

A cry escapes Scarlett's lips as another shot sizzles somewhere above us like a firecracker.

"GO!" she screams, dropping to her knees in the bow with both hands over her head.

This time, I don't hesitate. Engine sputtering to life, I shift the tiller forward, the boat lurching ahead so fast I almost stumble off my seat. The rumble of the motor grows louder, and my heartbeat grows with it.

Water stings my cheeks, my neck, as I point the skiff in the direction of a narrow channel, bouncing in time with the waves.

A second later, another shot rings out, coming from our left. I toss a glance over my shoulder, and that's when I see it, following after: a white center-console boat.

I can't discern the owner's facial features, just the figure of a lean man with a rifle in hand, aimed in our direction. Then a yellow flash, one after another.

A bullet strikes the boat, bouncing off the aluminum with a metallic clang. Another slug zips past my face, so close I can feel the heat skimming my cheek.

"Take my place," I shout, hoping Scarlett can hear me over the drone of the motor as I fumble beneath my seat for the pistol.

My fingers brush against metal at the same moment another shot ricochets off the stern.

I suck in a breath, take aim on the dark figure, and I fire.

There's the flash of the explosion from the muzzle as the gun kicks upward with violent recoil, followed by a booming sound reminiscent to the clap of thunder.

Yards away now, the center-console boat throttles back. Smoke lingers in the air like a gray cloud, and I can only hope the bullet somehow made contact.

Gun still in hand, I drop to my knees in the stern, gaze trained ahead, half-expecting the boater to round the bend and finish what he started. Trees race by in every direction, gnarled branches reaching for us in our escape.

With every twist and turn of the boat, my stomach clenches, head growing faint like it used to on that ride at the county fair—spinning too fast one minute, before jerking to the right, left, and then forward until I can taste the bitter acid at the back of my throat.

Beads of sweat form on my forehead. Black spots dance behind my vision.

Every flicker of movement from the shore—every falling limb or acorn—sends me in a panic. I grasp the pistol tighter as I brace for the next deafening shot. Once we've made it safely back to the entrance of Lost Lake a few minutes later, I finally let out a sigh of relief.

As I stand, my legs quiver. One hand gripping the gunwale, the other enclosed around the weapon, I manage to keep myself upright, aware of everything and nothing all at once.

Scarlett's arms circle my waist. The gentle tips of her fingers brush the strands of hair from my eyes. A moment later, her breath is warm against my cheek.

"It's okay. We're okay," she says.

"Do you mind telling me what the actual hell just happened back there?"

Scarlett takes a small step back, eyeing me for injury. "I think that's pretty obvious, don't you?"

"Enough," I say, and she flinches, those green eyes widening. "Cut the bull, Scarlett. This isn't a game. Our lives are at stake."

"Which is why you need to go." Even to me, the words come as a surprise. "It's not safe for you when I'm around. They're both looking for us now, which is why we need to split up. We need to go our separate ways."

"Go? Go where?"

She crosses her arms. "Don't you have somewhere to be?"

Bart's. Forget Bart's. "It doesn't matter. I'm not leaving you."

"Why?" Her voice loses its cool tone, replaced with a venomous edge. She needs to calm down or drop this until we can head inside, before she gives us away.

But her hands make contact with my chest, shoving me back. "Why can't you just go on home? Pretend like I never existed." Tears glisten in her eyes now. Harsh, angry tears. "I promise you'll be safer that way. You'll never have to worry about me or Mama ever again."

Turning on her heel, Scarlett steps out of the boat and onto solid ground, not even bothering to wait for me. She has every intention of leaving me here. To speak her peace and slam the door in my face, with the hope that I'll leave and never come back.

But to do so would be foolish. To do so would make me an equal to both of my parents—one who willingly left, the other who had no other choice—allowing Scarlett to become the next face flashed across the screen on the evening news, the next girl whose fate is whispered about like the result of some football championship or controversial church sermon; a tragedy to be consumed and recounted until the next.

"Let me stay here," I say, knowing she'd be crazy to turn me down after the danger we just escaped. "At least for one night."

Scarlett stops and turns to face me, arching a brow. "Wouldn't your dad get suspicious if you didn't turn up?"

"I'll text him. Tell him I'm staying the night at a friend's house."

Like I even have friends, I think. *Like Grandpa will even notice if I don't come home.*

"Good luck getting cell service," Scarlett says.

"Listen," I say, taking a tentative step forward, "you don't need to be alone. That wouldn't be smart. Someone literally just tried to kill us, and I wouldn't know how to live with myself if they got to you when I'm not here to keep you safe."

My pulse skips when Scarlett snorts, chuckling to herself. *What the hell?*

"What is it with guys and their brains that make them believe girls are so incapable? *Shit!* What do I look like to you? A girl who's never had to keep a box cutter in her purse or a gun under the front seat of her car just in case one of those men from the ring tried to take me? A girl who didn't keep pepper spray in her pocket at work in case one of the men from the bar decided they wanted to do more than just stare at my ass?"

My cheeks burn. I don't know what to say.

"Whatever," Scarlett mumbles. "If you want to stay, then I'm not going to stop you. But don't think for one minute that I can't fend for myself when that's all girls are trained to do since the day we're born." She stomps off, hands tucked beneath her elbows. When she reaches the door, she looks back at me and says, "Are you coming or what?"

I look down at my feet, thinking. "Where will I sleep?"

Scarlett doesn't waste a moment. "Not with me, if that's what you're hoping."

My gaze meets hers and then I can't hold it in any longer.

When a laugh escapes my lips a moment later, Scarlett just shakes her head. "What the hell is wrong with you?"

"Nothing." I step out of the boat and onto the dock, not even trying to hold back a grin. "But what is it with girls and their brains that make them believe they're such a catch?"

Scarlett waves a middle finger in my face, and I laugh again.

"Shut up and get inside," she says, opening the door a little wider. "*Now.*"

"Whatever you say, Scarlett," I mumble, brushing past.

Once the door closes behind, Scarlett sinks to the floor. Between her fingers, she whispers, "What do we do now?"

17

HIDEOUT

"**I**T'S A PYRAMID."

"What?"

"The girl from the river a couple weeks back; her tattoo was a pyramid. Did your mom have one since she used to be in the ring?"

We're sitting on the floor of Scarlett's houseboat, surrounded by empty cans of Vienna sausages and expired Spaghetti-Os. My stomach feels queasy and swollen.

I can tell by the startled look on Scarlett's face that I'm right.

"The police found a body a few miles down the river from here less than a month ago. The girl had a tattoo on her shoulder. At least, that's the talk. I'm guessing she was one of the prisoners your mom was trying to help?"

A mosquito whines around my face, but I swat it away for what seems like the hundredth time. I try not to imagine the other insects crawling or buzzing around the place, coming in through a cracked window or a slit in the roof.

"Her name was Emily," Scarlett says. "Emily Duggins. She was the last girl Mama tried to save."

"How did she end up at the river?"

Scarlett sighs. "Mama told Emily to meet us at Walmart. Then we went to the old fishing camp at Dead River. Mama told her specifically not to leave or talk to anyone but she didn't listen. When she didn't show after a couple days, Mama left to find her, said Emily had probably gone to get cigarettes or use a phone. I told her it wasn't safe, to be careful, but Mama refused to be cautious. She said to stay here and not come out for anyone. But after a while, I grew impatient. Next time I saw her, she was…"

"It's alright. You don't have to say it."

"The man in charge of the ring found us, Clay," Scarlett whispers. "The same bastard Mama was in a relationship with, before she found out who he was and what he was involved in. We ran once he found out that Mom was working against him, getting those girls to safety. But somehow, the bastard tracked us down. He found Mama, and he found Emily. Soon, he'll find me."

"Not as long as I can help it."

She shakes her head, locks of blond hair swaying around her face. "You don't understand. He's not the only one you have to worry about. God only knows how many people he's got looking for me, how many hours they've spent out here, or how many miles they've traveled up these creeks and sloughs trying to find where I am." Her gaze shifts to the .22 rifle hanging on the three wooden pegs above the door. "Good thing Mama came prepared."

"Let me help you." I shift forward until I'm close enough to reach out and touch her, bridging the gap between us; to let her know that I'm not giving up on her like everyone else gave up on me. "Let me talk to the police. They'll know what to do. We'll tell them about Emily, about your mom, and you can lead them to the ring. Then, you'll be safe, the bad men will go to jail, and the other girls can go free. Isn't that what you want?"

Scarlett brushes my hand away, drawing both legs to her chest. "No, Clay. Are you stupid? This isn't some Hallmark movie. They think I killed a man. If that detective wasn't lying, they might even have a warrant… for my *arrest*. That'll get us nowhere." With her head tilted forward and her gaze trained on her sandals, a thick curtain of straw-colored hair falls in front of her face. She looks wild, desperate—akin to a girl who's run out of options.

And in this moment, nothing I do or say will be able to change her mind.

"Besides, I don't care about going to the police right now," she says. "Sure, they might find those girls, but they won't find the man in charge of the ring. We've been on the run from him for years now, never staying in one place for more than a few months. Trust me: he's too smart to be found, always a step ahead. Right now, I only have one goal, and that's to stop him." Scarlett looks up from her sandals. "I'm going to kill that son of a bitch. He's ruined so many people's lives, Clay. I have no doubt he killed Mama and Emily, just like he plans to kill me. And whenever he shows up, I'll be ready."

Her words make me shiver. Instinctively, my gaze travels up to the .22 rifle again. I can easily imagine her holding him at gunpoint with it like she did with me. I wonder how long she might wait before pulling the trigger.

"You think the person who shot at us is the same man your mom hooked up with?" I ask. "The same man that's over the ring?"

"I don't know," Scarlett says. "I didn't get a good look at him."

"Why didn't you tell me any of this before?"

She sighs again. "I wanted to, Clay. I really did. But once I said it, once you knew, I couldn't promise you'd be able to just walk away. I didn't want to put you in danger. Besides, you seem like a good guy. Someone who deserves far better than this."

I inhale a quick breath, picking up one of the many cans scattered around our feet and tossing it up into the air.

You can't stay here.

It's not safe.

She's not who she claims to be.

The thoughts clamor around in my mind, lodging themselves inside my brain like sharp knives. I grit my teeth, hoping to God I'm not making a mistake with every second I spend in this place, sitting in front of a girl—who others might call a runaway—that I somehow know better than anyone else.

"I was foolish to think I was safe after what happened to Mama," says Scarlett. "Foolish to think I could pull you into this without one of us getting hurt."

"Scarlett. Don't."

"I'm sorry," she says, wiping her nose with the back of her shirt sleeve.

"You're not going to believe this," I say, setting the can beside me, "and I wouldn't expect you to, but I honestly think you're one of the best things that's happened to me."

There's an awkward pause. Finally, Scarlett says, "Oh, really? You mean getting shot at and almost killed is your sick version of fun?"

"Well, when you put it that way…"

Tugging on the cheap fabric of her threadbare sock, Scarlett blushes. "Just when I think I have you all figured out, you find some way to surprise me."

"That makes two of us."

Something twists in my gut, face burning with shame, with the bitter truth. There's no use keeping the verity of my situation inside any longer. Not after everything she's told me about her life. "Out there, in the real world, I don't really have much of anything. I'm not popular. I'm not the star athlete or the guy with twenty colleges beating down his door. I'm just a prime example of an average Joe. A guy who'd easily blend into a crowd unnoticed. In fact—"

"Clay, if there's something you need to tell me…" Her words trail away, replaced with the outside noise of water lapping against the bank and tree branches scraping against the aluminum roof.

After a moment, she says, "Would you believe me if I told you something?"

"At this point, I'll believe just about anything."

Scarlett forces a smile, but it's gone just as soon as it appears. "We moved so often that I never really had friends. Mama told me not to get too close to anyone. She didn't want them knowing our secrets, or how she was trying to help those girls."

Somehow, her words remind me of Dad the year after Mom left. Back then, we lived for the weekends, when Dad and I would load up for a day on the river, leaving everything else behind. We'd pack ham and roast beef sandwiches inside small coolers, consume unhealthy amounts of Mountain Dew, and tell stories while waiting for the fish to bite. At the time, Dad was the only person I could really count on. Not Alex from second period geometry, who made small talk feel like a chore once we figured out we had nothing in common. Not Kyle, who parked beside me in the mornings to chat before first bell and whose truck always reeked of weed. Not Bailey from lunch, going on and on about some guy she'd had a crush on since kindergarten while we waited in line.

None of them could relate to the simplicity of our river excursions and the comfort of speaking without saying a single word—an art Dad and I mastered after countless outings to the Choctawhatchee. No one else understood the anxiety of keeping friends after our trips to the river grew less and less and after my weekends were traded for a labyrinth of cold, sterilized halls.

I can't pretend to ignore the truth any longer: Scarlett and I are more alike than different. Both of us with a past so difficult we can barely speak of it without tearing up. The loss of a parent. The loss of innocence at an early age. Going on with our lives like every day isn't its own fresh version of hell.

Now I look up and say the words I've never been brave enough to say out loud. "I've never really had friends either," I tell her.

Later, after several rounds of Rummy and Blackjack using a deck of cards Scarlett found tucked inside a utensil drawer, and after the last of the sunlight begins to lose against its struggle with the darkness, we clamber on top of our bunks. The old bedsprings creak and moan beneath us, so loud I can't help but worry if they'll manage to give us away. But once we're still, all I can discern are the night echoes of the swamp—the steady chirp of crickets, the croak of rain frogs, the occasional bellow of an alligator, and the river, licking and tapping all the while against the side of our aluminum hideout.

For what feels like hours, neither of us speak. But just as I'm closing my eyes, seconds away from sleep, Scarlett whispers, "Clay, you awake?"

"Yeah," I answer back, practically jolting upright. The squeaking of the bedsprings gives me away. "Can't sleep."

"Just close your eyes and pretend you're somewhere different," she says.

And so I do.

I pretend I'm walking along the beach, hand in hand with Mom, our palms sweaty in the heat of the summer sun. I pretend I'm inside a plane, barreling higher, higher, as my nails dig into the armrest, watching the cottony clouds drift by outside my window and the buildings grow smaller beneath me.

"It's what always helps me. It's what Mama always said to do." As her words float down to me from the top bunk, I imagine her staring straight up at the ceiling, both hands clasped to her chest. "When we first got here, that was the only way I could get through the night, only way to force myself to sleep. I was so scared. But I was also glad because I thought we were finally safe. I thought this time would be different. It's so secluded out here, so isolated, but turns out that couldn't stop them from finding us."

"How long have you and your mom been on the run?"

"Nearly all my life, Clay. Nothing's ever been normal for me. As a child, I guess I just accepted the fact that Mama didn't like to stay in one place for too long, since I didn't know the real reason why she got a new job every few months. I only learned what she was really involved in when I was in middle school and eavesdropped on Mama's conversation with one of the trafficked girls over the phone. I'd heard too much, and she had to tell me the truth…had to tell me *everything*. Ever since, I've had to live constantly looking over my shoulder, paranoid that the guy from her past had found us."

"How did your mom know where to look for these girls?"

"There are dozens of them in the same ring all over the country. A lot of them work in bars or motels, and if you find one, you can find them all, because they're all like sisters. Some of them have to turn over a paycheck, some sell drugs, and some sell their bodies."

I squeeze my eyes shut, the visions of the beach and the plane ride replaced with the thought of beefy men with too-broad shoulders, slits for eyes, foul cigarette breath, and women whose skin stretches too tight over their bones, their bodies as pale and fragile as porcelain.

In my gut, I know she's telling the truth. In some way or another, those men and women exist, as much as I hate to admit it. I don't want to believe the world can be so twisted, so dark—that trafficked people can live so close without me even noticing them.

"When Mama worked in a bar, she would sometimes hire these girls," Scarlett says. "They grew to trust her and began sharing their stories. She helped some of them get out, but she couldn't help them all. Because of the risk of being discovered or one of the girls talking, we constantly had to relocate to other places. One tip from them, and the man over the ring could've easily tracked us down."

"Why didn't your mother go to the police? Couldn't they have worked with her to help save these girls?"

"No, Mama didn't trust the police. She said it was too risky, that the ring had too many people working for them, possibly even members of law enforcement. And if the bastards got word that we were cooperating with the law, they would just kill all the girls and start over somewhere else.

"The women kept their mouth shut too. Didn't breathe a word to anyone, 'cause they didn't think anyone would believe them. When I worked at the seafood joint, I overheard the men at the bar calling the women Mama hired skanks and lot-lizards. Said they hustled to get extra change. And the local police in and out of the restaurant paid these women no mind, almost like they weren't there."

"But if they told the truth, someone would've believed them, right?"

"Telling the truth is different for these women," Scarlett says. "They're looked at as lowlifes and trailer trash. Everyone thinks they're full of shit."

"I don't think that."

"Be honest. If you crossed paths with one of them, you would care enough to hear them out?"

As soon as the words leave Scarlett's mouth, I'm reminded of her mother that day at Bart's, how I'd taken note of the woman's balled fists and pale skin and that paranoid glint in her eyes—one that seemed to cry, *Help me.*

How I'd turned away, annoyed, and didn't say another word.

"See? That's what I thought," says Scarlett.

Something wet trickles down my cheek. "I'm sorry. It's not fair. I wish I had a better answer—wish I could do *something*."

If Scarlett hears me, she doesn't let the words stop her. If anything, she uses them as fuel, like a tape machine that won't stop until its run straight out of reel. "I got to know a few of the women Mama helped. Some had cigarette burns and bruises, and were so skinny you could see their bones; others looked like they hadn't slept in days. Most of them refused to make eye contact and struggled to make conversation. Mama said it's hard for them to know how to act around someone who's not controlling them."

While Scarlett talks, I flip onto my side and stare at the wall. It's hard to believe that this is the life for so many people. Of course, I've heard of human trafficking before; I know it's a real problem. But I never thought it would lead to the river, much less a place as boring and dull as Delton. In fact, a few days ago, the river was my bubble from the outside world, edging out everything painful and dark. Now, I realize how foolish I was for believing the river could shield me from danger. I'm nowhere near as safe out here as I thought.

"…Mama says the traffickers can find you anywhere too," Scarlett drones on. "At the movies. The park. Even took one kid from the arcade… caught him at the slot machine and offered to pay for more tickets while his parents waited in the parking lot. One of the girls told Mama about him. Said it's likely he'll never see his parents again."

Scarlett keeps talking and I struggle to stay awake, my eyes feeling heavier by the second. I'm almost asleep when she calls out my name in the dark, her voice small and delicate, sounding nothing like the girl from a couple days before.

"Clay?"

"Yeah?"

"Thank you. For staying."

18

TELLTALE SIGN

WAKE TO SEARING light and an imposing certainty—*Bart's. I'm late for Bart's.*

The thought sends me in a flurry of panic, stumbling out of the scratchy, cotton sheets and bounding for the little round table where I left my phone the night before.

I've never been late. Not once in almost two years of working there.

As I power on my phone and check the time onscreen, one thing becomes definite—Lynn will be pissed.

"Clay? What are you doing?"

Scarlett stares back at me from the top bunk, dark purple bags beneath both eyes like she hadn't gotten any sleep. Her gaze drifts from my face to my bare chest, and then all the way down to my feet, her pale cheeks instantly turning two shades darker.

And that's when I realize why.

"*Oh*—I'm…it's not how it looks."

Scarlett turns away, but not before I notice the dopey smile stretching across her face.

Here I am, with a girl I've only known for a few days, standing in nothing but my boxers, expecting her not to notice.

"Oh, God. I've got to get going."

Tugging on my jeans and quickly looping my belt through the rings—both cheeks burning—I gather up my phone, wallet, and cap as fast as I can.

If I leave now, maybe Lynn won't scold me as bad. A stern word or two versus a sit-down with Bart himself.

"Clay...*Clay*, wait!"

There's the creak of bedsprings and the patter of feet across plywood. Arms wrap around my chest as I reach for the doorknob.

"Please, please be careful," she mumbles into my back, with her face pressed against my spine. "I'll see you later?"

If my cheeks were red before, they're scalding now. "Y-Yeah. Of course. I'll be here."

Scarlett lets go, taking a step back. "Good. Maybe we can talk about how pitiful our lives are again some time." Then, noticing my hand grasping the door knob, she adds, "If you want."

"Sure. But let me bring the snacks," I say, glad to change the subject. "If I ever eat another can of Vienna sausages again, it'll be too soon."

"Clay? One more thing?" she calls out once I step onto the dock.

"Yeah?"

"Don't worry. I've seen worse." She winks.

My heart sinks, and I feel my cheeks grow even more flush. "See you later, Scarlett," I mumble.

"You sure you've never had a girlfriend?" she asks, making me stop again.

I shrug. "None that count."

Both arms crossed, she stands inside the doorway now, smiling playfully. "That's what I was hoping."

She's closing the door when I say, "Scarlett?"

"Yeah?"

"I promise we'll get through this. One day, this'll all be different."

Her smile fades. "I appreciate it, Clay. I really do. But like Mama used to say, nothing's ever been easy for us. I don't expect for it to start now."

This time, she shuts the door in my face without another word.

I know she's watching from the front window as I leave, which is why I wait until I've rounded the bend and am well out of sight before I dig the wallet out of my back pocket.

Not mine, but *hers*.

Even in my panic, I hadn't hesitated to grab both from the little round table before she could notice.

The leather is tiger print, cracked and weathered from years of use. Inside, I find her driver's license, a Starbucks gift card, fifty dollars in cash, and several loose coins.

Scarlett Anderson is the name printed on the Florida driver's license, the listed date of birth confirming she's eighteen—a year older than me.

Which means she hadn't lied about her identity. The girl in the photo even shares the same green eyes and smattering of freckles across her nose as the teen Detective Conaughey showed me yesterday at Bart's.

Maybe Scarlett's right and cops like Conaughey lie because it's what they're trained to do. But if Conaughey lied about something as simple as her name, then who's to say I can trust any other word that comes out of his mouth?

I close the wallet and place it back in my pocket, relieved to know that Scarlett was telling the truth for once. Still, why do I get the sense that I only know the half of it?

As the boat gathers speed, seeming to glide across the surface of Lost Lake, I can't help but wonder what else Scarlett isn't telling me.

There's one other vehicle at the boat landing besides my own—a black SUV with tinted windows. It's parked conspicuously, taking up two parking spaces, almost as if the driver's waiting for someone.

After securing the boat to the shore, I keep my gaze trained ahead, all too aware of the gun clipped to the waistband of my pants, just in case the same person who shot at me and Scarlett the day before decides to show up again.

The hairs on the back of my neck stand on end—a telltale sign that I'm being watched.

Scarlett's words replay in my mind, stuck on a loop. *He found Mama, and he found Emily. Soon, he'll find me.*

I only make it a few steps before the driver's side of the SUV glides open. Still, I don't wait to see who it might be. Head down, with both eyes trained on the pavement, I climb into the truck, slam the door, and shift the vehicle into gear. But just as my foot nudges the accelerator, he steps into my path, forcing me to brake.

For a second, all I do is stare, both palms slick with sweat.

I know this man.

"Clay?"

He steps around to the driver's side, taps on the window glass.

"Clay," Detective Conaughey repeats, once the glass slides down and the humid, outside air rushes in. "Thought I might find you here."

"Is there something wrong?" I ask.

He smiles. "Just wanted to follow up. Checking to see if you've given any thought to what I said." Detective Conaughey motions behind us, to the expanse of muddy water stretching through the trees. "You haven't seen that girl anywhere, have you?"

"No, I haven't." My gaze snags on his wrinkled, white-collared shirt, the first few buttons undone to reveal a tanned, hairy chest.

His eyebrows cinch together. "Sure about that?"

"I'm positive."

"Let's hope so, but I was your age once too. Lied my way out of most things. My first joint. First speeding ticket. First time sneaking out. I had damn near everybody fooled."

"Oh, yeah? What changed?"

I expect him to pause, take a moment to mull things over, but instead, he says, "I grew up. Learned to tell the truth, take my punishment like a man. I'm not sure if anyone's ever told you this before, son, but nothing good ever comes from lying. There are consequences when you don't tell the truth, lies that can upend the rest of your life. This is one of those times."

The truth is a slick, writhing fish, impossible to grasp. Can he tell I'm lying? How much does he already know about my trips to Scarlett's houseboat and Dead River, or the abandoned hunting camp where she'd shown me the list of prisoner's names, stuffed in the floor of a damp, dark houseboat?

And, even more important: Can I afford to give my secret away?

I think of Scarlett's wallet in my pocket, the proof that could help make him believe me, trust me.

"How much does the truth cost?" I ask, watching the corners of the detective's mouth twitch as he considers what I'm implying.

"$5,000, if your information leads to anything substantial."

A cash reward, in exchange for what I know. After all, I could use that money. It would help Grandpa. Help pay off the debt from Dad's medical bills, countless chemotherapy treatments, and even pay for some new fishing equipment.

In the end, is all of that worth more than Scarlett's safety?

"I wasn't lying when I told you the first time," I say, readjusting my cap out of habit before placing my trembling hands back on the wheel. If he can tell how anxious I am, he doesn't show it. "I haven't seen her. But thanks for letting me know how much she's worth."

The detective's eyes narrow. With a tip of his head, Conaughey mumbles, "Alright, kid. That's it. That's all I needed to know." He reaches inside his pocket. "Still got my card?"

"Of course I do."

Detective Conaughey glares a second too long. "Well, if you think of anything that could help, I trust you'll let me know."

He slaps the hood of the truck as he turns to leave, making me jump. "See you around, Clay."

I draw in a shaky breath and nudge the gas pedal, telling myself not to look back.

But as I head to the landing to load my boat, I feel his eyes on the back of my head, watching me go.

19

A LITTLE SECRET

IF **DEALING WITH** Detective Conaughey made me nervous, the thought
of facing Lynn is just short of a full-on panic attack. I can't afford to
lose my job. Not now that Scarlett and Grandpa are among my top
priorities.

As I step through the entrance, that tiny bell clanking against
the glass and confirming my late arrival, I inhale a deep
breath and force myself to take whatever punishment
Lynn has in store.

She's hunched over the register, counting
out a stack of bills. Head down, muttering
beneath her breath. "$67, $68..."

I clear my throat, making my entrance
known. "Sorry I'm late."

Lynn doesn't look up, hands smoothing out
several dollar bills before placing them back in their
correct spot. "$71, $72..."

I swallow, though my mouth has grown noticeably dry.
"Lynn."

"One moment, Clay. Can't you see I'm working?"

The question doesn't sting as much as it should. In fact, it comes out as more of a harmless jab.

Lynn slams the register shut, and I jump. Her green eyes focus on me.

"I'm sorry," I blurt, at the same time she says, "Ms. Judy called."

For one long, uncomfortable moment, we stand in silence.

Her mouth twitches. Both nostrils flare.

Here we go, I tell myself. *Here it comes.*

"What're you sorry for, kid?" she asks, crossing both leathery, sun-tanned arms over her chest. "Being a half hour too late? I get it. It happens."

"Where the heck is Lynn, and what have you done with her?"

I can clearly recall a past employee who'd forgotten to lock the cricket cage door, leaving the critters to roam throughout the store overnight. The next morning, Lynn made him collect as many of the active critters as he could, snickering like it happened all the time. After, she called him back into her office, and I never saw the poor fellow again.

Now, she sighs and says, "Look, I know you have a lot on your plate. Between your grandpa and your dad, it's more than any guy your age should handle. Especially by himself."

That's not the half of it, I almost blurt, but I grit my teeth to keep from saying anything I'll regret later.

Two times now that Lynn's left me off the hook. Two times that I haven't had to own up to any consequence.

"Just don't let it happen again," she says, turning away to begin the next task off her daily list of chores.

"I'm sorry. It won't happen again."

Lynn picks up a broom, swatting at a cobweb over her head. "Good. 'Cause whenever you don't walk through those doors like you're supposed to, all I do is worry. Can't even be mad, I'm just...on edge."

The comment hits me like a gut punch. Lynn...worried? About *me*? "Well, there's no need to worry. About as much good comes from that as those cigarettes you're always smoking."

Lynn playfully swings the broom at my face, missing me by a couple inches. "Alright, boy. Don't make me change my mind. Get to work, or get out."

"Yes, ma'am," I say, stifling a chuckle.

"Clay?" she asks, the instant I turn in the direction of the bait shop.

"Yeah?"

"Are you sure something else isn't going on?"

My face falls. I can't help it. Do I really make it that obvious?

"Like what?"

Somehow, I know exactly what she's going to say. "It's because of a girl, isn't it?"

Heat floods my cheeks and my pulse quickens. Slowly, I turn back around.

How much does she know?

"Come on," she laughs. "You think I wouldn't notice how shady you've been lately? It's just not like you."

"Sure," I snort. "Like I've always been an open book."

"No, that's not my point, kid. It's more how quiet it is now when you're around. Even more so than last year, when everything happened with your daddy. These past few days, you've had this sneaky look in your eyes like you're hiding something. And you're always checking that phone."

I scrunch my shoulders. "It's not what you think."

"Oh, yeah? Then if it isn't a girl, it's something else. Something worse." She props the broom against the counter, taking a step closer.

I stare down at the tops of her scuffed Asics, the truth seconds away from slipping out.

And when it comes, I don't fight it. Not anymore.

"Her name is Scarlett," I whisper.

Silence. Louder than the whirring of my own heart.

But I can't take it back. It's already too late for that.

"Scarlett," Lynn breathes, as if saying the girl's name aloud somehow makes her real. "What a lucky young lady."

I clench my teeth. Force a smile. One to fool her into believing that I'm okay, that there's no reason to worry about me anymore.

Lucky. If Scarlett's anything, she sure isn't lucky.

Unfortunate, maybe. Miserable. Possibly even cursed.

But that's one secret I'm willing to keep.

Ms. Judy answers on the second ring. I call her back from the parking lot a few minutes after my shift's end, away from the ever curious, skeptical Lynn. I can't trust she won't read too much into our conversation, worrying even more about me than she already is.

"Clay." Ms. Judy sighs. "I almost didn't recognize your number."

"I'm sorry I missed you earlier. Trust me, I haven't forgotten."

Her voice sounds distant, as if she's holding the receiver too far from her face. Either that, or the result of bad reception, which makes me have to strain to hear her words. "I was hoping you hadn't. But I hate to be a bother. You must be real busy."

"Always," I groan.

"Got any big ones for me? You know how much I love those filets."

"I'm sorry, but no, I just haven't had the chance this week. Time's been getting away from me."

A beat of silence, before her faint voice drifts through phone static. "Well, that's not like you, dear. But don't mind me. I'll catch you when things start to wind back down."

Guilt churns in my gut. All of this running around, darting back-and-forth between work, the river, and Lost Lake has caused me to lose track of customers like Ms. Judy, straining not only my time, but my income.

I can't afford to lose this. Not after I've worked so hard.

"It's my fault," I say. "I have to do better. There's no excuse for it."

"Now, there's no need blaming yourself. I know enough about you to know you're a hardworking young man. Not many of your kind left, I'm afraid." She sighs again, her breathing more labored than before, as if she's struggling to put her feet up in the recliner. "Let me let you in on a little secret," she says, and I can imagine her covering her mouth and whispering into the receiver, even though she's the only one there. "Sometimes, it's not even about the fish. It's more or less that I just need someone to talk to."

"I understand. Everyone gets a little lonely."

After all, isn't that why Scarlett always seems excited to see me? Why she's always begging me to stay? Is it loneliness that keeps her from running me off, or something else?

"Tomorrow," I tell her. "I can take you to the river tomorrow, if you're up for it."

I can practically hear the spirit returning to her voice. "Of course! I'll be ready whatever time you show up. Anything beats sitting here in this recliner all day. Enough to drive me crazy. And, Lord knows," she says, chuckling to herself, "I don't need to get any crazier."

"Alright. Tomorrow it is."

"Tomorrow," Ms. Judy says, before the phone clicks and she's gone.

20

GONE FOR GOOD

I **HAVEN'T BEEN HOME** from Bart's five minutes when there's a knock on my bedroom door.

"That you, son?" Grandpa's voice sounds from the other side.

"It's me. You can come in."

"Dinner's ready," he says.

"Alright. Be down in a minute."

To be honest, the thought of Grandpa in the kitchen makes me more anxious than relieved. Typically, I'm the one in charge of preparing the meals, even though most nights that means swinging by to pick up a pizza on the way home.

The last time Grandpa attempted to cook, I intervened before he could add a jar of strawberry jam into a boiling pot of spaghetti. "It's all in the sauce, son," he laughed at the time. In my heart, I knew his jest was only a failed attempt to play off the embarrassment of what he'd been about to do.

Today must be one of Grandpa's better days—one where he

can remember the responsibilities handed down since Dad's passing. Still, I know it won't last. Every day is a different battle. One day I'm a stranger to him, the next some friend he had in high school but lost contact with over the years.

It's only a matter of time before his memory's gone for good.

"Where have you been?" Grandpa asks, eyeing me as I inspect the meat sizzling on the stove.

After giving everything the once over—pork chops, a pot of turnips, a plate of fried cornbread, fresh out of the grease—a breath of relief escapes my lips.

If I had any optimism left, I might believe things were heading back to normal.

"I was at work."

"But…but last night…" I turn, watching Grandpa's gaze grow distant, like glass. If I hadn't witnessed it before, I'd think he was just distracted. "Last night, you weren't—"

"I was at the river."

After all, it's not a lie. But even more surprising is how he can recall my absence when he can barely remember to take his daily meds, or, worse, gets dressed for church on any other day but Sunday.

Is it possible he notices more than I know?

"The river," Grandpa repeats, after I've prepared both of our plates and we're seated on opposite sides of the dining room table. A pang of regret forms in the pit of my stomach for leaving Grandpa alone the night before. I should know better. I'm all he has left.

I stab a piece of pork with my fork, staring at it absentmindedly. "Thank you for dinner," I say, even though my mind is somewhere else.

"Let me tell you a story," he says through a mouthful of turnips. Juice trickles from the corner of his mouth, catching in the white stubble along his jaw. "One night, I was fishing out near Mile Lake, just minding my own business. It was dark, black as a cave. Not a star in the sky." His eyes widen, and he crosses both arms with a slight tremor. "All them swamp noises were giving me chills. You could hear the crickets and rain frogs and the loud screech of an owl flying overhead. All of a sudden, I heard a scream on the other side of the bank. Almost sounded like it was coming from a little girl. After I got through shivering, I laughed. Told myself, 'Just one of them wildcats.'"

He wipes a napkin along his chin, folding it and then placing it back in his lap. When his eyes settle on me again, he says, "A minute later, I heard it a second time. But it wasn't a scream of fear. It was a cry for help."

Grandpa scoops up another spoonful of turnips, chewing them until his gaze settles on the dining room wall behind me, staring at the map of the Choctawhatchee River system.

"Grandpa," I say. "Aren't you going to finish your story?"

"Huh? Was I saying something?"

"Yeah. You were telling me this story about a little girl at Mile Lake—"

"Oh, yeah!" He snaps his fingers, a string of turnip dangling from his bottom lip. "That little girl yelled, *'Momma! Momma, come back!'* Let me tell you, I about pissed my pants." He chuckles to himself, staring down at his bowl of greens.

"Who was it?" I lean closer. "Did you ever find her?"

"Aren't you hungry?" Grandpa points to my untouched plate. "Look at all that food. You better get to eatin'."

"Her name. What was her name?"

His forehead wrinkles, both eyebrows scrunched together. "What do you mean, son?"

"The little girl. The one at the river! You said you heard a little girl."

"What little girl?"

"Just forget it," I say, snapping a piece of cornbread in half out of frustration. "I'd never heard that one before. And God knows how many river stories you've told."

"The river," Grandpa says. "That reminds me…have I ever told you the story about the night I fished out near Mile Lake?"

"Lord help me," I mumble.

Halfway through his story, Grandpa loses his train of thought. But this time, I don't bother asking anything more on the subject of the little girl.

After we finish, I rake the remaining pieces of pork from our plates into the trash, placing both dirty dishes in the sink. Then, I bring Grandpa his cane and help him to the recliner.

"Thank you, Jason," he says, plopping down with a sigh. "How about bringing me my tea?"

Jason. Dad's first name. Every time I hear it, my chest constricts, and my breathing hitches, if only for a second. Grandpa's occasional slip-up with our names shouldn't catch me off guard, given the amount of times I've been called Jason the past few weeks, but it does.

It's Clay, I want to say. *Clayton Thomas, your grandson.*

It seems like the more I correct him, the more agitated he gets, shaking his head and repeating the name until he inadvertently forgets. As I've been told by doctors of dementia patients, there's nothing worse than constantly reminding someone of their faults, and so, I've had to learn to refrain and bite my lip whenever Grandpa displays clear signs of obliviousness.

I pour Grandpa another glass of iced tea from a pitcher in the fridge, and once I return, I find that, in the few precious seconds of my absence, he's retrieved a gun.

A 12 gauge shotgun, to be exact. Grandpa always keeps it nearby, in a different spot every week, in case of an emergency. I used to worry he would accidentally shoot me, himself, or fire a round off in our house until I removed the firing pin so that it wouldn't shoot. Taking the gun away would have been too traumatic for him. Now his paranoia is more of an annoyance than anything. I've learned to let him be and wave it around until the episode passes.

"They're coming, Jason," Grandpa whispers.

The name makes me wince. "Who?"

"The bad men. And when they do, I'll be ready."

"Why would they come here?" I ask.

"Because they know I'm onto them. They know I've figured out their plan."

"It's late, Grandpa. How about we watch the episode of *Swamp People* I recorded last week? Then it'll be time for bed."

"No, no"—Grandpa shakes his head, gripping the barrel of the gun so tight his fingernails turn white— "there's no time. No time at all. They're coming. The bad men are coming…"

The bad men. Isn't that what I'd called the people Scarlett's convinced are looking for her?

I shake my head. It's nothing but a coincidence. Most likely, Grandpa's confusing the past for the present again, mistaking a few high school bullies or drunks as a current threat. Either that or the government, coming to take his guns away.

There's just no telling with him anymore.

"Goodnight, Grandpa," I say, stifling a yawn as I head in the direction of my room.

"Goodnight, Jason."

Thirty minutes later, after I'm almost certain Grandpa's asleep in his recliner, I retrace my steps back to the living room. As expected, his eyes are closed, mouth agape, a line of drool trickling down one corner of his mouth. Every few seconds, a small snoring sound escapes his throat.

Carefully, I remove the gun from his hands, which fall slack onto his lap, and prop the shotgun against the wall in a far, shadowed corner. But before turning out the lights, I tiptoe to the edge of Grandpa's recliner and bend down to kiss him on the cheek. "Goodnight," I whisper.

"They're coming," he mumbles, so soft I almost miss it.

Then, a moment later: "Don't worry. I'll keep you safe."

With a sigh, I turn away, even if some part of me wishes to stay, listening to catch some hint to his past while he dreams. I shouldn't think too much about it. He probably can't even remember what he had for dinner. But somehow, just like Scarlett, I can't help but wonder how much I really know about the man I call Grandpa.

21

SUSPICION

A T SIX THE next morning, when the sound of my truck rolls to a stop in Ms. Judy's gravel drive, she's hobbling down the porch steps with a bottle of sunscreen in one hand and a can of bug spray in the other.

By 6:30, after a slight detour to pick up several biscuits at a nearby Piggly Wiggly, we're pushing off from the boat landing, headed downriver in my Jon boat.

Ms. Judy sits with both hands tucked beneath her thighs, a few breadcrumbs from breakfast clinging to her cheeks. With a small grin and a peaceful glow behind her eyes, the eighty-year-old woman marvels at the sight, a straw hat pulled down to the tips of her ears and a plastic windbreaker hanging off her shoulders a few sizes too big.

Though I can barely recall Grandpa's last trip here—I always mean to take him along, but somehow never find the time—I remember his stories of their summers spent along these banks as teenagers, wild and unbridled, free of parental supervision. Images come to mind of him and Ms. Judy's flawless golden tan from hours spent beneath the sun every day, skin-tight swim wear, and bare feet pounding the sandy bottoms of bone-dry creek beds. Then, days of building forts in the oppressive July heat, spotting for swimming holes, and sharing kisses beneath the shade of a palm tree out of sight of the other neighborhood kids—a predictableness to it all that never grew old. It was in those times, Grandpa once said, that life was its own slice of heaven. After all, those summer months served as a temporary reprieve from school and seasonal chores, the lives of Grandpa and Ms. Judy like Tom Sawyer and Huck Finn. All the while, he said, the river was a place of mystery and myth, of freedom and solitude, where one couldn't help but feel like an orphan in a different world, belonging to everything and nothing all at once.

At the thought, a familiar loneliness tugs at my heart, aching for a relationship—someone to laugh with, touch, and share this constant coldness in my chest—and the childlike innocence of running barefoot through these swamps just like the people before me all those summers ago.

Now, I imagine how the place must look to someone like Ms. Judy, the landscape barren and bleak after sixty-five summers without her, trees stunted in growth due to the numerous hurricanes, floods, droughts, and tornadoes over the years. As a result, the overhead limbs now bear the shape of the wind, the bank eroded and boggy, with multiple man-made items caught in the snags along the shore—fishing line, a board or two from an old dock, a piece of rope, an empty beer bottle.

But there's also something serene about it all, to the fingers of fog sneaking through the leafy foliage, hovering like damp breath; the sweet and spicy smell of milkweed and traces of pollen coating the calm surface, each breath of wind shedding yellow dust.

We tie off along a clump of cypress knees, our lines swishing over the rusty-brown surface. Ms. Judy doesn't even ask for help, flicking her wrist back and aiming for a narrow spot in between two fallen limbs, the movement like muscle-memory after all this time.

After several minutes, the conversation from the night before still weighing on my mind, I dare to break the silence. "Did Grandpa ever tell any crazy stories about fishing on the river at night?"

"He did," Ms. Judy says abruptly. "But most of them didn't make any sense, even before his dementia."

I pluck a cricket from the cage resting on the gunwale, the insect writhing and tugging in my firm two-fingered hold. "What about with Dad?"

"Well, now that you mention it, Jason and your grandpa did come home one night acting sort of strange. It took a while to get anything out of them. I could tell they were real shook up."

"Do you know why?" I ask.

"Unfortunately, I don't. When I asked about it later, your grandpa told me to never bring it up again."

"And that didn't make you curious?"

"To be honest, I didn't worry much about it. He was always acting like that, mostly kept to himself. I knew if something was bothering him, he'd tell me."

"But he never did?"

She sighs, looking away off the side of the boat. If I didn't know any better, I'd think she was hesitating to answer. "No. Never. And your father was the same way. Who knows how many secrets those two kept to themselves over the years."

"Secrets? What kind of secrets?"

Ms. Judy turns to look at me, both eyebrows pinched together. "What's gotten you so interested, son? Your grandpa hasn't told you anything, has he?"

I swallow, focusing on the cricket still squirming in my grip. The creature's hind legs kick outward, itching for escape, as I impale the hook into its soft underbelly. "He mentioned a little girl, heard her screaming somewhere near Mile Lake one night. That's all I could get out of him before he blanked."

"Doesn't ring a bell," she mumbles, shaking her head. "But I guess we all have our secrets."

The words lodge themselves inside my brain, making the skin on the back of my neck tingle. "Yeah," I say, turning away before she can notice the color drained from my cheeks. "I guess so."

If I'd found Scarlett, who's to say Grandpa hadn't discovered another girl?

Like me, who's to say he'd tell anyone at all?

An hour later, with six bream in the live well and an enthused Ms. Judy, we decide to spot out another location a few paces down from our current fishing hole, hoping for a bigger catch.

This time, I tie us off on a submerged limb as we stop to rest in the shade. With my pole baited and cast, I dig around in a small cooler beneath my seat for an ice-cold Mountain Dew and a pack of peanut butter crackers.

I hand a soda can to Ms. Judy. "I've missed this," she says, in between sips.

"You should get me to take you more often."

"Don't want to invite myself," she says, with a wink. "You don't know how much this means to me, Clay. Can't even tell you the number of times I worried I'd never get to come back here. When you're old like me, you'll realize most everything you do as a child trumps everything that comes after."

"That's what Grandpa says, too. He can tell just about any story from childhood and those summers he spent here with you, but can't remember much of anything that happened in the past twenty years. Guess it's a good thing," I say, my thoughts drifting to Dad and dark hospital rooms, and Mom, with her watery echoes in my dreams at night.

Ms. Judy snorts. "Lord knows all the mess he's told about the two of us. Sad thing is most of it's true. I'd go back in a heartbeat if that meant one more day on this river with him."

"What happened?" I stare deep into the trees that shelter the shore, imagining younger versions of the two hand-in-hand as they traipsed through the forest, leaves crunching underfoot; the soles of their feet growing darker, dirtier, with every step across mud. "What changed?"

We were always friends, Grandpa told me once, back when he still had most of his memory. *Took years for us to make up our minds and act on it. By that point, I'd already married and divorced Jason's mama. We waited most of our lives to even decide what we knew all along.*

"Life is messy. Oftentimes, things happen that you'd never expect. And that…that was one of them." I tear my gaze from the tree line just in time to see Ms. Judy wipe a stray tear from her cheek. "I loved that man more than anything. Trust me when I say that was the toughest decision I've ever had to make."

"Did he do something to you?"

She sighs. "No, it's just that sometimes people change."

When another tear trickles down her cheek, I wish I hadn't asked anything at all. "Oh. We don't have to talk about it if you don't want to."

"No, it's fine. Really. It's just…I don't expect anyone to understand why things ended the way they did. That's only ever been between us."

And now Grandpa can't even remember, I remind myself, but I don't say it out loud.

Suddenly, there's a violent tug on Ms. Judy's line, the pole moments away from slipping into the river.

"Oh!" Ms. Judy yelps, snatched forward.

Crossing the boat in two assured strides, I bend down to her height. "Do you need help?"

"Hurry!" she squeals in a shrill voice. "Take it! I'm not strong enough."

I do as she says, gripping the pole in both hands and rocking back on my heels, straining on the line.

"You got it, Clay?" she asks, hand on the small of my back. "Can you tell what it is?"

I smile at her. "Think we've got a catfish."

After wrestling with the catch for nearly ten minutes, the fish tires out.

"You want to try and lift it?" I ask her, to which she nods and reaches out with two wrinkled hands.

"Sure, but only if you help."

"Careful," I say. "Don't tug the line or the hook will slip from his mouth and he'll get away."

Following my directions, Ms. Judy lifts, lips pursed in a determined grimace. My hands cover her own, keeping the line steady just in case she loses control.

In a spray of water and a hiss of breath, the channel cat emerges gleaming wet, skin slick as oil.

"Ain't he just beautiful," Ms. Judy trills.

"Hold on," I say, reaching into my pocket and extracting my phone. "Let me get a picture."

Pole in one hand and the line with the fish dangling on the end clutched in the other, Ms. Judy poses for the camera, lips pulled back into a gummy smile.

"How's that look, son? Don't tell me I'm frowning."

"Of course not. It's perfect."

From the looks of it, the catfish appears to be about two pounds, the head as big around as a fist and whiskers close to three inches in length. Placing the phone back in my pocket, I follow my usual method by gripping the catfish's head tight with the spines between my fingers, removing the hook with the other hand.

Just as I'm closing the lid of the live well, I notice my own pole propped against the stern. It's bent in a familiar arc. Line taut as a bowstring. Mere seconds from falling overboard.

Something's hooked on the end. Something big.

With a terse pull, the line breaks with a snap, sending the bobber and hook flying into the fingerlike branches overhead. Ms. Judy emits a startled yelp, the noise echoing across the expanse of water and wood, sounding out the mumbled curse beneath my breath.

Standing on the bow on tiptoe, I reach up into the limbs as far as I can stretch, ignoring the scrape of a branch against my cheek and the foliage brushing along my skin.

My fingers wrap around the trunk of the tree, keeping me in place.

One hand on the trunk, the other gripping the broken fishing line, something catches my eye, blending in with the surroundings.

Something out of place. Something that doesn't belong.

Ms. Judy's voice sounds from somewhere behind. "Clay, be careful."

Ignoring her, my gaze focuses on the square object strapped around the tree a few inches above my hand. My fingers run along its camouflage face, with one lens like a Cyclops's eye. It's plastic.

This time, Ms. Judy's words drip with suspicion. "What did you find up there?"

Pulse quickening, I whisper, "It's a camera."

22

A CHANGE OF SCENERY

WE STAND IN the center of the boat, our necks craned and attention diverted to the game camera I'd unclasped from the tree only moments before.

Ms. Judy's voice is careful yet full of warning. "If it doesn't belong to you, shouldn't you put it back?"

Sighing, I lift my gaze to hers. "I would, but don't you think it's a bit creepy that whoever set this up is also taking pictures of us?"

"And? What could they possibly be—"

She pauses midsentence, realization flashing behind her silver eyes. "Here," she says, holding out a veiny hand. "Mind if I have a look?"

I oblige, the camera slipping from my grip as she gives it a quick once over.

Then, without a second's hesitation and a mere flick of her wrist, she tosses the object into the river.

"Hey! What was that for?"

"Sorry," she says, one hand over her mouth to suppress a snicker. "I've always had a problem with nosy people."

"Didn't you at least want to know what was on the SD card? We could've figured out who set it up in the first place."

She swats around her face like she's waving away a fly. "What you don't know can't hurt you, son. Best to just leave it alone." She stabs a finger in my chest. "That's good advice. Remember that."

Clapping both hands together, Ms. Judy continues. "Now, it's time for something different. Perhaps a change of scenery. Up for a little exploring?"

I scratch the back of my neck, my voice laced with frustration. "Sure. I guess so."

"Good. As long as we stay away from Dead River."

"Why?"

She shrugs. "Brings back too many memories."

"I didn't know you knew about that place—"

"Yes. A little too well, in fact."

When she doesn't elaborate further, I ask, "Did something bad happen there?"

She smiles, but her voice is cold. "What was that advice I gave earlier? Best to just leave it alone."

For the rest of the excursion, Ms. Judy remains silent, failing to offer up any more secrets or hints to the past. At Mile Lake, I expected a smile to push through her solemn expression, or some flicker of memory to appear behind her eyes, but she remains imperturbable. Even at Two Sisters junction, which I'd known Grandpa to mention on more than one occasion, she appears unfazed.

The only inclination that she's not about to fall asleep are her eyes, scanning the sides of the bank, the tops of the trees, and then back down to the water, as if in search for something.

It makes me wonder, if only for a moment, why else she asked me to take her along.

By midmorning, the sun beats down on us with an unflagging fury, driving out the chill from a couple hours before. If anything, the humid June air confirms the beginnings of a cruel summer climate. Turtles and gators emerge dripping wet from the murky depths to rest on logs or submerged limbs the same dusty hue as fossilized dinosaur bones. Somehow, the seasonal ritual feels oddly prehistoric.

For a while, we stick to the places of Ms. Judy's childhood, ones easily identifiable on a map of the Choctawhatchee River system, like the one displayed back home on the dining room wall. Any thought of Scarlett is quickly dismissed. I can't afford to reveal her location. Not after the promise she vowed me to keep.

But deep down, I know there's no way I'm ever going to get away with such a secret for long. It's only a matter of time before someone stumbles upon Scarlett or Lost Lake, and it's only a matter of time before I'm reprimanded or, even worse, arrested for my involvement with a so-called fugitive.

After all, the river never keeps its secrets for long. *Secrets always surface,* Dad used to say.

Questions gnaw at me, nagging like pesky insects. Can Ms. Judy provide any indication of who Scarlett might be? Might she know of the girl's mom or a distant relative, see a trace of them behind Scarlett's eyes?

A resident of Delton for as long as I can remember, Ms. Judy must know everyone to ever step foot in the place.

The possibility is almost too much to bear. After all, can I trust her to keep this to herself? It's not like she gets out much; just like any other senior adult, her most frequent stops consist of the local Piggly Wiggly and Sally's hair salon.

With my mind made up, I point my skiff northeast, in the direction of Hidden Creek. The route is so much more familiar to me after this past week that my hands have somehow memorized every turn, knowing just when and where to steer to avoid any objects obstructing the path.

Before long, after veering right into an even smaller canal, the boat is skimming across the water, and the channel widens into a vast region of towering trees and sparkling green water, which encloses all around like a giant fishbowl.

"Welcome to Lost Lake," I say over my shoulder, echoing Scarlett's words that first time she brought me here.

"It's beautiful," Ms. Judy replies. "How in the world did you find it?"

"Pure fate," I lie.

Soon, after a few more twists and turns around winding bends, I catch sight of Scarlett's Jon boat tied to a clump of palmettos next to a floating, pockmarked dock. The windows of the houseboat are dark, the entire structure cast in shade, providing the impression that no one's stepped foot in the place for years.

I would think the same, if I hadn't already spent a night inside its grimy walls, trading secrets in the dull glow of lamplight.

Between a stab of regret and an anxious bundle of nerves in the pit of my stomach, I resist the urge to throttle the engine and turn back around, before Scarlett's world collides with that of a stranger once again.

"Ms. Judy," I say, motioning toward Scarlett's houseboat, "there's someone I'd like for you to meet."

23

OLD NEWS

THE DOCK CREAKS beneath my weight with every step. "Scarlett?" I call out.

She's not waiting for me like usual. I'd expected her to be sitting with her feet hanging off the dock once she heard the familiar sound of my engine. But, oddly enough, she's not here.

"Scarlett?" I call again.

Everything's too quiet, like the very place itself holds its breath at our presence. No chirp of crickets from the trees or cicadas in the branches overhead. Just the sound of my heart beating faster, louder in my ears.

"Everything okay?" Ms. Judy pipes up from inside the boat.

"One sec." My fist pounds on the wooden door. Once. Twice.

The knob turns, the door slipping open a crack, as a hand clamps onto my arm and pulls me across the threshold.

"Who is that?" Scarlett hisses in my ear.

For a second, the flurry of movement catches me off guard.

But then I notice the .22 rifle propped within reach against the closest wall, just out of Ms. Judy's sight.

I grit my teeth. "No," I say. "That's not a good idea."

The hand around my arm squeezes tighter, her nails digging into my flesh. "Who is she?"

Alarm sets in with the pain, and I tug away from her, rubbing at the red marks where her nails have scratched the skin. "Calm down," I whisper, even though I want to scream at her for even considering shooting an old woman. "She's just a friend."

"But...but I thought..." Both eyes wide and manic, Scarlett paces in the entranceway, casting occasional glances through the crack in the door. "I thought you didn't have friends."

Times like this I can't help but wonder how well I really know her. Getting worked up to the point of contemplating violence—especially against someone as diminutive and docile as Ms. Judy.

"I wanted to introduce you to an old family friend. Someone who might be able to help." I sigh, running a hand over the bill of my cap.

"I already told you. I don't need help," she says, crossing both arms.

I glance at the weapon. "I can see why."

Scarlett snatches the gun up, and I take another step in the direction of the door. After all, how much can I really trust her? I thought I could. I thought we'd grown past the fear and awkwardness that once resulted from the two of us together.

But the cold glint in her eyes and the way she hesitates before rising on tiptoe to place the rifle back in its spot above the doorway makes me reconsider everything.

Then again, maybe it's my fault for breaking our promise. For bringing someone here knowing the consequences that Scarlett's acute paranoia might cause. For making her believe she can trust someone, when after eighteen years, she's only ever trusted her mother and her gut, acting on instinct rather than emotion.

"I promise, Scarlett. You can trust me. I wouldn't do this if it didn't help in some way."

"Whatever," she grumbles. "Let's just get this over with."

Ms. Judy watches as we emerge from the houseboat, Scarlett two steps behind the entire way across the dock to where she waits, inside the boat now parked ashore next to Scarlett's skiff. "Ms. Judy, this is Scarlett. Scarlett, this is Ms. Judy."

"Hello, Scarlett," Ms. Judy says, holding out a hand.

"Hey," Scarlett says back, both arms crossed. Not even an attempt at a smile.

After a moment, Ms. Judy tucks her hand back beneath her thigh, her grin attempting to absolve the awkwardness of Scarlett's social skills. "Are you friends with Clay?"

"Yes, ma'am," she says, even though both cheeks flush red at the indication of those words. "Just friends."

"I see." Ms. Judy stares a second too long, her gaze skimming over Scarlett's disheveled hair, flimsy flip flops, baggy jeans, and wrinkled T-shirt. "Quite a place you have here."

"Yeah. Belonged to my mom."

Ms. Judy's eyes widen. "Is she here?"

Scarlett doesn't even flinch. "No. She actually just left a few minutes ago. I'll tell her you asked."

"Oh. And what is your mother's name?"

Scarlett stiffens. "Why do you want to know that?"

"Just to match a face to a name, I suppose. Lived here all my life. Know just about everybody."

"You wouldn't know Mama. She's not from here."

With a tilt of her head, Ms. Judy says, "Is that her houseboat?"

"Yeah."

"I see," Ms. Judy says again. "Well, it was nice meeting you, Samantha."

"Scarlett," I say. "It's Scarlett."

"Right," Ms. Judy laughs, shaking her head. "Of course it is."

Scarlett looks down at her feet. "I'll be back tomorrow," I tell her, but she doesn't say anything else. In fact, she won't even look in my direction. Her hands tremble by her sides, her flushed cheeks now drained of color, but I'm too afraid to ask what's wrong.

"Enjoy this weather, dear," Ms. Judy says, once we've pushed off from the bank, drifting back the way we came. "And watch out for that alligator there."

Just like before, the creature watches from several yards away in a shallow, weedy patch of the swamp. It'd be easy to miss if not for the gator's rounded snout and brown, scaly head floating slightly above the surface.

"Big Al's no problem," Scarlett says, still staring at her flip flops. "Isn't causing me any harm."

"Has he been around for a while?"

"Yeah. Always in the same spot."

"Well," Ms. Judy says with a click of her tongue. "Seems like Big Al might have babies. Watching us out of protection for her young. Most female gators build this giant nest of detritus and vegetation and bury their eggs there. They might guard it for a few months."

"As long as I don't bother her, she won't bother me," Scarlett says.

"That's right. It'd be a bad decision to approach her."

"How do you know so much?" For the first time, Scarlett looks up, her hardened gaze flicking to mine and then back to Ms. Judy, like the two of us are strangers. "He bring you here often?"

"Oh no," Ms. Judy laughs, raising her voice as we drift farther away. "Used to come here as a girl. Stayed for weeks at a time. Just like you."

As we near the bend, the houseboat beginning to slide from view, Ms. Judy waves back to her, but Scarlett doesn't even bother returning the gesture.

Instead, for one tense second, her gaze locks onto the woman's back, steely and unflinching. A sharp, private look.

Then, she pivots, slinking back to her lonely little refuge.

I turn my attention to Ms. Judy, who's staring down at the water now, as if lost in thought. "Have you ever seen her before?"

"No," the old woman says. "Never."

But there's something about the slight quiver in her voice and the way she refuses to look me in the eye that makes me think she's lying.

An hour later, the sights of the river replaced with the pale-pink walls and disarray of Ms. Judy's living room, she sighs from the comfort of her recliner, feet propped up with a crossword puzzle book resting across her lap. "You have no idea how much today meant to me, Clay."

"We'll have to go again sometime," I say, even though my gut tells me I won't be taking her back to Lost Lake anytime soon. I'd left the place with more questions than answers, ones about Ms. Judy's past and the strange interaction between her and Scarlett. Some part of me can't wait to see Scarlett again just to ask her what, if any of it, meant.

"That girl…"

"Scarlett."

"Yes, Scarlett. The two of you close?"

"Not in the way you think. Not like you and Grandpa."

"Really?" Ms. Judy licks her fingers, flips the page of her crossword book. "With a little makeup, and the right pair of clothes, she'd be drop dead gorgeous. I don't exactly blame you for trying."

"I'm not sure she's into that sort of thing," I say, silently wishing we could be talking about anything else. "Besides, I'm probably not even her type."

"No need to be so insecure, son. You could have any girl you wanted."

"Not true, but thanks for the confidence. Besides, I don't want just any girl."

"Right. You want *her*."

Ms. Judy tucks a pencil behind her ear, closing her book, and peering at me through a pair of outdated spectacles resting on the bridge of her nose. "Watch out for that girl. Something mighty odd about that whole situation." She reaches for the remote amid a mess of cookie crumbs, peanut remnants, and silver Hershey's Kisses wrappers on the nightstand beside her recliner, powering on the TV. "There's been too many dead girls found out there along that river. Lord knows we don't need anymore."

"Don't worry. Scarlett can keep herself safe."

Onscreen, a local news anchor rehashes the same old news from this morning for the same faithful midday viewers, failing to provide an update on the case of a conservative congressman awaiting trial for links to a sex-trafficking ring. At the news, I bolt upright in my seat. Could this congressman be involved with the same ring that Scarlett's mom helped those girls escape from or the same one she was caught up in herself all those years ago?

The camera pans to an older woman with salty-gray hair and dark skin sitting inside a coffee shop. I recognize her from the political TV ads that play at night whenever Grandpa's watching cable. "As long as people keep defending these politicians, refusing to accept that the case is legitimate, and continue to make excuse after excuse for their party's underdog, then no one will ever be able to get to the truth," she says, to the applause of several baristas behind her. "He may be guilty. He may be innocent. We won't know until the jury decides for themselves.

"It's a shame this mess still happens," she continues. "And I'm sick and tired of seeing people in power who ought to know better involved in the middle of it. But it ought to serve as a clear reminder to the residents throughout this county that the ones in charge of our care and general well-being allow this to take place without proper oversight. Talk about hypocrisy. Where's the safety in that?"

"Damn right," Ms. Judy says from her recliner, once the camera snaps back to the same monotone news anchor. "No one's safe anymore, which further proves my point. Hard to trust anyone when the ones in charge can't even keep it in their pants." Lowering the volume, Ms. Judy shakes her head. "I could tell that girl's been through hell. Don't know quite what, but it's something. Something bad. And she needs someone to trust. Someone to believe her." Ms. Judy motions to the screen. "She won't get it anywhere else."

I think of the list of names scrawled inside that notebook and stored beneath the floorboards of an abandoned houseboat along Dead River. I think of Scarlett's words: *The women kept their mouth shut…didn't breathe a word to anyone, 'cause they didn't think anyone would believe them.*

"Would you believe her," I say, staring at the photographed face of the congressman onscreen, "if she told you everything she's told me?"

"I believe I would," Ms. Judy says, her words strangely distant, eyes wide in a far-away gaze. "More than you know."

24

IN MY BLOOD

T'S NOT CURIOSITY this time but suspicion that has me standing in front of Grandpa's map on the dining room wall. Suspicion stemming from Ms. Judy's words earlier this morning and the mystery they posed.

As long as we stay away from Dead River. Brings back too many memories.

Perhaps it's nothing as significant as my own secret. The ominous atmosphere of the place might be enough to explain away Ms. Judy's reason for steering clear of the area.

But to be fair, I'm not entirely convinced.

I trace my finger from Mile Lake to Dead River, two locations that have been shrouded in mystery this past week by the two people who most likely know the river system better than anyone else.

Right away, I notice something. Something strange.

An orange push pin, inserted in the place of each location.

Grandpa. He must've remembered something. It's the only explanation.

After all, it can't be a coincidence. Not after what Grandpa said about the little girl screaming for her mama one night at Mile Lake or Ms. Judy's insinuation that something bad had taken place at Dead River all those years ago.

The only question is: How are the two related?

The next morning, we sit in silence on the edge of Scarlett's dock, our toes skimming the surface. It's been five days since I found her mother's body. Five days since becoming involved in this web of lies and peril. Five days of knowing Scarlett.

She won't look at me, and I can tell by the firm set of her lips that something's bothering her.

"Listen, about yesterday…"

"You shouldn't have brought that woman here," she says, like a parent reminding a child of their mistake. "That's all I've got to say about it."

"I know, I know. I just thought she could help. As a family friend—"

"I don't care who she is, Clay. It's not safe." She rubs her bloodshot eyes with the back of her hand, slumping against me when she's done, her head resting on my shoulder. "I can't keep this up much longer. I thought the man who killed Mama would've found me by now or I would've found him. All this sitting around and waiting feels pointless. Maybe if I leave, he'll find me sooner, and this can all be over. But then where will I go? Once I kill that bastard, what happens after that? And if I stay here, then what's the point? Mama's not coming back. And one day, I know you won't either."

"Don't talk like that," I mutter, but she goes on anyway.

"One day, you'll move off to college, find some girl who treats you better, and you'll forget all about this place."

"How could I? I'd have to be pretty heartless to walk away. Especially with everything you've told me. I wouldn't give up on you like that."

"Anyone else would."

"But I'm not anyone else. Why leave when I've got everything I need right here?"

Closing my eyes for a moment, breathing in the sweet, smoky scent of cypress with the warmth of the sun across my face, I add, "The river's always been like home to me. Most of my good memories are here, with people like Dad and Grandpa. And now I'm sharing those memories with you."

"I just don't want to be holding you back," she says.

"Maybe you can't tell, but I'm not like everyone else. All my classmates dream of leaving the first chance they get, but I haven't thought that way in a long time." I pick up an acorn from the dock, tossing it and watching the tiny ripples emerge as it impacts the surface. "I used to, though. There's a sort of power in leaving everything you've ever known. It sounds freeing, at least for a while. But I won't be the one to break tradition. Leaving's just not in my blood. I have to stay. For Dad. For Grandpa. Even for Ms. Judy."

"I guess I'm just surprised. Most everyone I knew in school couldn't wait to move off. They didn't even know who they were or what they wanted to be but they knew it wasn't in their heart to stay."

"Most people are like that. Have to 'sow their oats' as Dad called it before they can settle down."

"Yeah, well, I still haven't found my home. Most days, I feel like I have no purpose other than to mess things up and ruin shit. I have no idea what I'm supposed to do now or who I'm supposed to become. For the longest time my goal was just to lay low and help Mama from being found out. But one thing led to another, and now I feel as trapped as I did back then.

"Sometimes, though, when it's dark out, and all I can hear are the sounds of the river at night, sometimes I tell myself I can live here. And then people like you come along that make staying seem easier."

I can't help but think back to the nights of endless tossing and turning after Dad's death, wishing for something different—someplace away from the reminder of his room at the bottom of the stairs, or the dining room table he'd never eat at again or the couch he'd never sit on watching endless reruns of *Breaking Bad*.

Then I found Scarlett, her very existence enough to keep me tethered, consolation in knowing that others were worse off.

"Don't worry about me," I tell her. "I'm not going anywhere."

She nods, but there's a slight hesitation to the gesture, in the way she lets go an audible sigh of relief. "I just get so, so lonely. So scared. And then I get to thinking about how *all this* might be too much for any other person to handle. Almost like, every time you leave, I convince myself it's the last time I'll see you."

I think of my mother, that crate balanced in her arms as she leaned down to whisper in my ear. *I'll be back soon, Clay.*

Dad, and the foolish promises he made, like the cancer would magically go away with rest and time.

Now, I touch a forefinger to Scarlett's chin and raise her face to meet mine.

"I could never leave you," I whisper.

When I stand to leave, only thirty minutes to spare until the start of my morning shift, Scarlett stops me with a question. "Do you remember what Ms. Judy called me? Right before both of you left?"

Noting my silence for confusion, she says, "Samantha. She called me Samantha. But that's Mama's name."

"It was a mistake," I say. "A little slip-up. It has to be."

"No. No, it can't be. Not if she recognized me. Not if she knew Mama and put two and two together."

"But you said it yourself. Your mother wasn't from here."

"Unless that woman saw Mama at the river before."

"But that's not—" I shake my head, Scarlett's words refusing to sink in. "She told me she hasn't been here in years."

"What if she lied?" Scarlett says.

"Ms. Judy wouldn't lie."

Scarlett crosses both arms. "When's that ever been true about anybody?"

"I'm just saying. She wouldn't do that."

With a shrug, Scarlett says, "Maybe you don't know her as well as you think."

25

CONSPIRACY

IT'S BEEN ONE week since I last stepped foot inside Delton Café, even though it'd be foolish to believe anything's changed in the days since. The fifteen cars parked out front of the diner confirm the congregation of men already packed inside, most of which haven't skipped a breakfast here since President Nixon was in office.

Delton is a town of tradition, and it's evidenced here by an establishment that's never been renovated and whose owners consist of the next son, daughter, or grandchild in line of the family business. The white paint is old and dated, the pictures hanging along the walls faded and blotchy, and the artificial daisies adorning the tables should've been thrown out years ago. But with everything that's happened this past week, its predictability is comforting.

Gravel crunches beneath my feet along the path to the screened-in front porch, the air smelling of fried bacon and smoke, floating above the place in a gray haze. I used to go to the café with Dad every Friday morning before school, a tradition lasting from the age of four to my sophomore year, when Dad's cancer raged the worst. We'd share bowls of steaming hot cheese grits, split mounds of chocolate-chip pancakes, and sneak bites of golden hash browns fresh out of the grease off of the other's plate, always leaving with our jeans a little tighter. It was the highlight of my school week, an occasion that never grew old.

Now, the place feels a little emptier, a little smaller with the both of us missing from our window seat in the front of the café. I catch a glimpse of the corner table through a part in the curtains. The very sight of it makes a lump form in my throat, spurring a fresh wave of nostalgia.

A bell clanks against the glass as the door closes behind me with a shudder, the noises within the cramped space suddenly too loud, too forced. There's the screech of fork tines against glass dishes, bacon crunching between teeth. Snatches of whispers and murmured gossip drift back to where I stand beside the register, akin to a stranger now without Dad, lost within an environment of surly old men; ones whose arthritic, trembling hands clutch sweaty glasses of iced tea, their blood-flecked eyes tossing occasional glances in my direction.

The only reason I dare step foot in this place is because of the sealed bag of catfish filets in hand, which feels heavier by the second.

I can do this, I tell myself, walking past the cluster of tables and the group of senior's random chatter. Gary, with the same worn-out camouflage cap; Charles, with a white ZZ-top beard in desperate need of a trim, and James, whose black sunglasses suggest a past career as a secret service agent.

I know all of their names, just as they know mine.

"Clay," a familiar voice shouts from the end of the table.

It's Charles, a couple drops of yellow egg yolk caught in his beard.

"Hey," I say, forcing a grin. Ten heads swivel in my direction. "Haven't seen y'all in a while."

"What's biting this week?" Charles asks, peeling open a biscuit and smearing grape jelly along the insides with the blunt end of his pocket knife.

"Mullet mainly. In fact, I got an extra bag if any of you want some."

"Catch me next week," Gary pipes up, adjusting his cap. "Knowing Lucy, she'll have it on the menu before breakfast's over."

I nod, wave a hand in parting, and head for the swinging kitchen door as Delton Café's only waitress, Dinah Campbell, barrels through at almost exactly the same speed, plates of hash browns, sausage, and scrambled eggs balanced along both arms.

"Excuse me there, Clay," she says. "Good to see you."

"You too," I say, but among the bustle and noise of the place, I doubt she even heard.

One of my faithful customers, Lucy Partridge—current owner and cook—wipes her hands on her apron as I stumble into the kitchen, taking the bag from my hand before I even have a chance to speak. Her abundance of black eyeliner and a set of grinning teeth always remind me of a raccoon. Today, sweat gleams on her brow from the steam hanging in the kitchen.

"My God, son. You've grown another inch."

Adjacent to a gas stove, multiple glass plates line a prep table. A black cast-iron grill—the centerpiece of the kitchen—sizzles as bacon and sausage patties fry atop the scalding surface. The arrangement of meat and fried eggs look like chaos, and I always wonder how Lucy manages to keep it all straight.

"It's only been a week," I say before Lucy pulls me in for a bone-crushing hug. Her hair and clothes reek of grease and smoke, hands sticky with pancake batter.

"You know I lose track of time. Memory ain't the same as it used to be."

When she lets me go, I notice a familiar look cross her eyes.

Pity.

"I've been meaning to call, but things have been so crazy."

I lean against the prep table, watching Lucy multitask like a juggler in the circus, flipping eggs with a spatula, adjusting the heat dial, feet tapping all the while to the faint seductive voice of Conway Twitty on a radio above the prep station.

"Heard anything new about that body down at the river?" I'm certain she's only changing the subject so we don't have to mention Dad.

"The one from a month ago? No. Not really."

As the kitchen door swings open, I catch snippets of conversation coming from the old men's table—this morning's deliberation involves the Water Wars with Georgia—before it swings shut again, the voices diminishing to a low hum.

"It's all anyone wants to talk about," Lucy says. "That and some perverted politician charged with ties to some sex-ring down south in Miami. Heard anything about that?"

"Actually, I have."

"Crazy world we're living in, son."

"…he's got a wife and kids," Gary explains, his voice drifting back to us as Dinah hurries inside the kitchen again to retrieve the rest of their order. "Sounds like them democrats are just trying to ruin him."

"Everyone's got an opinion around here if you can't tell." Lucy winks. "Guess what? So do I. Those men are lucky I keep my mouth shut."

"What do you think?" I ask, desperately wishing for a change in subject. "About all those women's bodies found along the river? Coincidence or not?"

Lucy plucks an egg from a white carton, cracking it on the edge of the grill. "I don't believe in coincidences," she says, tossing the broken shell in a small garbage can by her feet, "but I think everything happens for a reason, even if it can't be explained."

"So you think the cases are connected or the victims are related in some way?"

"I think it's hush-hush on purpose," Lucy explains. "With what's happening on the news, the conspiracy theorist in me wants to think the government's involved. You can't tell me that's not the case when no one's ever caught their killer."

"There could be more than one."

"And they could be members of that sex-trafficking ring. Just saying."

The real question that's been gnawing away at me since I heard about the congressman awaiting trial is how many more people are involved in profiting off of prisoners like the women Scarlett's mom helped? Is this why these women rarely speak up? Why they rarely go to the police because members of the ring could be anyone and anywhere? Take the congressman, a man who develops and votes on legislation, introduces bills, and is supposed to serve the people. In reality, isn't he only serving himself?

The hypocrisy of it makes my head hurt.

Lucy scoops two fried eggs and several pieces of bacon onto a plate, handing it to me. "Alright. Breakfast's ready."

"You really didn't have to," I tell her, even though I take the plate anyway, an unspoken barter for the catfish.

She pokes a finger into my ribs, flashing a sneering grin. "Need some meat on them bones, boy. Now hush and get to eatin'."

I'm not even halfway finished with my meal before Dinah pokes a head through the kitchen door and shouts, "Lucy! You ain't going to believe it."

"What now?" Lucy grumbles beneath her breath.

"A body," Dinah says, her forehead glistening with beads of sweat. "They found another body down at the river."

My fingers tighten around the glass plate. "When?" I say.

"This morning, I 'reckon," Dinah shouts over her shoulder, retreating back to the dining room.

Lucy shakes her head, pinching the bridge of her nose. "I can't believe it. Now, we were just talking... *Clay?*"

Out of the corner of my eye, I notice her watching me, her gaze traveling down to my trembling legs. Turning on my heel, I practically push the half-eaten plate of eggs and bacon into her hands as I say, "I have to go."

"Clay? What's wrong?"

Into the dining room, the creak of the door swinging back and forth behind me drawing the attention of all ten men, already abuzz with the information, the truth glinting in their eyes.

Sucking on a cube of ice, James says, "Who would've ever dreamed..."

"...bet it's another one of them prostitutes," Gary replies.

I rush past them, lengthening my stride to the entrance.

"Hey, son! What's the rush?" one of them says to my back.

"Clay?" I catch a glimpse of Lucy bounding through the revolving door, the shadow of her hourglass figure stretching across the floor. *"Clay!"* she yells through the din of the room, but it's too late.

I'm already out the door.

26

DEAD OR ALIVE

THE NEXT TEN minutes are a blur of noise and color and panic.

Dinah's warning, playing on repeat in my mind: *They found another body down at the river.*

Scarlett. It's my only thought. One that latches on and won't let go.

Something salty and wet trickles into my mouth, clinging to my lips, dripping from my chin.

"I'm sorry," I whisper. "I'm so, so sorry."

I'm halfway to the river when another sob tears through me, the pain stabbing and raw. It reminds me of the day of Dad's funeral, when I knew there was nothing left to do.

I punch the dash, ignoring the ache in my fists and the reverberation of a scream ripping from my throat.

She's gone.

And it's all my fault.

Wind roars in my ears as I race to Lost Lake. Adrenaline keeps me alert, focused. *No distractions*, I tell myself. *No room for mistake.*

I have to find Scarlett, dead or alive. Even if that means exposing our secret. Even if that means undoing everything Scarlett worked so hard to keep between the two of us.

I can almost imagine the cuffs clamped tight across my wrist and the stern command that I have the *right to remain silent* as I'm shoved into the back of a police car for my involvement with a wanted criminal. But for once, I don't care.

As long as Scarlett is safe. As long as those men never touch her.

Several yards into Hidden Creek, a man in a green law enforcement uniform stands inside his boat at the noise of my motor. He calls out to me once I've slowed to a considerable pace. "You fish out here often, son?"

I bite my lower lip, attempting to calm the emotions coursing through me. "I do."

"Oh, yeah? When was the last time?"

"I catfish somewhere along here every day," I lie. Any other week it'd be the truth.

"Hey, I know you. You're that Thomas boy."

"Yes sir."

"Well, Mr. Thomas, you haven't seen anything suspicious, have you?"

I swallow the lump rising in my throat. "No sir. Why? Did something happen?"

The game warden points behind to the yellow crime scene tape strung across a small clearing of dirt and underbrush. "You can say that. We found a body that's probably been here two weeks."

My heartbeat slows. I bring a hand to my cheek, weak with relief. *It's not Scarlett.* "My God," I say, a second later. "Was it one of the old men who fish up this way?"

"No. Appears to be a female. About all I can say." He tips his head, holding up a hand. "I'm going to make a note in my book that I talked to you. We might have questions later down the road. Be careful now."

If only he knew. I wave goodbye, pretending not to notice him staring after me as I slip from sight.

Samantha. Scarlett's mother. The river had spat her body back onto the shore like the whale with Jonah.

A little part of me feels closure knowing that the warden uncovered at least some of her remains. Proof she wasn't just the figment of my imagination. Proof that the woman I'd spoken to in Bart's that day was real. Proof she'd once been Scarlett's constant, her daughter's entire world.

Proof that the river never keeps its secrets for long.

"We have to go." I stand halfway across the threshold, keeping an eye out behind me as Scarlett gathers her things.

"They found her? They really found her?" she asks, grabbing a black garbage bag from beneath the sink and stuffing random objects into it.

"Yes," I say. "Someone must've noticed the buzzards. Can't think of anyone who'd bother traveling this far."

"But I can't leave." Scarlett stops, the garbage bag now lying next to her feet. "I have to find the man who killed Mama, or else he'll never be caught."

"If you stay here, you're not any better off. It's only a matter of time before the police stumble across this place. We don't have much longer anyway. Don't want the game warden getting suspicious."

Several seconds later, between a string a curses, Scarlett mumbles, "I never thought it'd come to this."

I don't tell her that I suspected it would from the beginning. That her secrets—*our* secrets—wouldn't remain that way for long.

Just as the door clicks shut behind us, Scarlett grips my elbow. "My gun," she breathes. "I forgot my gun."

"Leave it. There's no time." She doesn't budge, so I take the bag of items from her hand and give her a soft push. "You have to trust me. Now *go.*"

This time, she complies, but I can tell by the time we've reached the boat that she's deciding against it.

I point to a plastic red tarp bundled beneath my seat. "You'll need to hide under that until we get to the landing."

"I'm not sure about this, Clay."

"You have to be. It's the only way." I pull her to my chest, resting my head on hers. "Trust me. Please."

Her body quivers. I wonder if she can tell I'm just as scared. "I don't want to end up like her," she murmurs into my shirt.

"Like I'd let that happen…"

I squeeze my eyes shut. *Even though I almost did.*

When she pulls away, I notice the tears forming in her eyes, threatening to spill over. She blinks, but I reach up and wipe a tear away before it can slip down her cheek.

"You have to be brave," I whisper.

The same thing Dad told me as he held my hand from his hospital bed, optimistic until the end. *Things will get better. I know it might not seem that way now…*

You're just saying that! I'd cried into the covers that reeked of cleanser. *You don't mean it.*

"Okay," she says, blowing out a shaky breath. "I'll try."

"Good. That's what I want to hear."

I wouldn't lie to you, Clay, he'd said, as I continued to cry, the bedsheets soaking up my tears.

But he *had*. He did.

In fact, things had only gotten worse. Grandpa's dementia. The endless tossing and turning at night when I should be asleep.

If it weren't for those words, maybe I would have believed after all.

But when Scarlett grips my hand, raising my chin to look her in the eye, I wonder if Dad was right. If Scarlett herself is the answer I've been waiting for.

She closes the gap between us, hesitating just a second before her lips brush against mine. My hand reaches behind her neck, pulling her closer.

For a second, it's as if nothing else exists but us.

And then, just like that, the moment is over.

She places a palm on my chest. "I'm ready."

27

DEATH WISH

PURPLE STORM CLOUDS clot the eastern sky, pulsing with light every few seconds. With any luck, the game warden will have already abandoned his post.

A thin layer of mist hovers above the dark water. My gut tells me that in less than an hour, the swamp will be completely drenched. I toss a glance back over my shoulder at the ruffled red tarp draped over Scarlett's form in the stern. If I stare long enough, I can make out the indentation of a body beneath the shabby fabric, though a passerby wouldn't be able to locate the tarp on the floor of the boat. She's hidden. For now.

Remaining in the middle of the waterway, I spot the warden's skiff and then his stout figure through the trees, the neon-yellow tape fluttering in the strong breeze behind his back.

"Stay safe, Mr. Thomas." His husky voice drifts back to me as he raises a hand over his head. Then, like an animatronic, he turns back to face the mound of dirt where Samantha's body was found, not giving me time to respond.

My once pounding heart now amounts to a dull throb in my throat, made all the more calm by the memory of Scarlett's lips pressing gently against mine. I hadn't been expecting it. Until a few moments ago, I might have continued to believe that she thought of me as nothing more than a friend. But maybe Ms. Judy was right. Maybe the signs had been there all along. If so, what other hints has Scarlett left for me? What other clues have I been too naïve to see?

"You okay?" I call back to her at the mouth of the river, the water before me swifter and more dangerous, though I know well enough which floating logs and branches to avoid on my way back.

I still for several seconds, waiting. Each moment she doesn't answer increases my apprehension. "Scarlett?"

There's the ruffle of plastic, and then a head emerges from beneath.

"We're forgetting something," she breathes, sitting up on her knees, the tarp wrapped around her body like a blanket. "The book. It's still at Dead River. We have to go back."

Of course. The page of names. One of the only links to Scarlett's life before.

I point the boat east, in the direction of the incoming storm.

"Alright, just stay down," I say before throttling the engine, sending us bouncing across the choppy current, not a second to waste.

I know all too well that the river is the last place to be during a thunderstorm. The lightning, the wind, and the pelting rain have been known to sink and drown many a river man through the years, which is why driving straight into one seems like a death wish.

But we have no other choice. If the book ends up in the wrong hands, those girls may never be found. And who would believe me otherwise?

Less than ten minutes later, the breeze is now a steady gust. I grab the rope clipped to the bow and pull the boat onto the bank of Dead River.

Scarlett stands, the tarp falling in a heap at her feet. "Hurry," I tell her.

The place might be eerie in the day, but it's even more frightening in the midst of a pending storm. The black trees—charred by a forest fire many years ago—bend and creak in the howling wind. In fact, the entire swamp *feels* alive, the trees swaying back and forth, squeaking like a worn-out porch swing or rickety picket fence.

"Hurry!" I yell this time, but she's already disappeared inside the last shack, the door banging shut behind.

I check my phone. Count to twenty. Repeat.

What's taking so long?

Why hasn't she found the book already?

With each second, I'm tempted to abandon the boat and race for the shack myself, waiting out the storm inside. But the moment I make up my mind, tossing a leg over the side, Scarlett appears, bounding down the steps.

"Did you find it?"

She's by my side in seconds, doubled over and gasping for air.

"What's wrong?"

Breathless, she runs a hand through her windblown hair and curses. "It's gone," she says, looking back at the shack and then back to me. "The book is gone."

"What do you mean *it's gone*?"

"I don't know! He must've found it."

"Who?"

"I don't know, Clay," she says again. "Probably the same person who shot at us. Probably the same person who found Mama."

Something tells me she knows exactly who that might be, but I don't have time to press further. "Listen to me. We'll find it. There's no need to panic—"

A crack of lightning arcs above our heads and Scarlett emits a high-pitched yelp.

"Dammit, Clay! What do we do?"

I sneak a glance at the sliver of purple sky through the tops of the trees. "We need to get inside, somewhere safe. Let's check in the other shacks. Maybe we missed something."

Not wasting another second, we bound to the safety of the first shack, avoiding the same busted beer bottles and Bud Light cans as before. Thunder precedes the explosion in the sky, shaking the ground beneath our feet.

Fresh cigarette butts litter the ground. If I didn't know any better, I'd think someone visited recently. Maybe the same someone who found the book.

The wind snatches the door from my hands and pounds against the wood siding. I struggle against the strong gust to pull it shut.

Inside, Scarlett trails a finger across the dusty floor, searching for a loose plank or secret hiding place. I choose to search the only other room in the nondescript, vacant hut of wood, one hand enclosing around the old brass doorknob. With a twist and a rush of breath, I yank it open.

Dust motes linger in the air, as well as the overpowering smell of decay. A dead rat, if I'm lucky. Fingers crossed it's not another body.

I press my finger over the flashlight feature on my phone until a stream of pale light illuminates the small closet. Holding my breath, I grudgingly step inside.

Something crunches beneath my foot.

A rat's carcass, as expected. Long dead and splayed on its side, one beady eye still open.

I stifle a grimace, directing my attention to the tiny storage space, crammed full of cardboard boxes, stacked one on top of the other.

"Hey, Scarlett. I think I found something."

The rain begins to fall, striking the aluminum roof, but I can still distinguish the creak of floorboards as Scarlett rushes to my side.

"What? What is it?"

"Old photographs. Lots of them." I meet her gaze. "Watch out for the rat."

"God, I honestly thought that smell was *you*."

I turn back to the open box on top to keep from punching her in the shoulder.

The photos are faded and blotchy; the images too grainy and dated to even make out the simplest of features.

All except for one.

It's an image of a woman and a little girl, whose small arms are wrapped around the woman's waist, cheek pressed against her side. They're sitting on the front porch steps of a shack, possibly the same wood hut we're occupying now. The woman—pixie-cut hair, narrow waist, wide hips— appears to be in her late 30s, early 40s. The girl can't be more than ten.

"I know her," Scarlett says, the edge of her finger brushing the side of the little girl's face.

A dimple digs into the side of the girl's left cheek, features sharp and pointed.

The resemblance is almost uncanny.

"It's your mother," I breathe.

"Samantha," Scarlett whispers.

Several words are written across the back—*Dead River. Summer of '86.*

The date makes my mind race. "You said your mom used to come here as a kid?"

"She did. But I don't know who she's with in this photo."

"Maybe it's an aunt. A distant relative. It couldn't be her mother."

Their features are too opposite, too contrasting. Still, there's something familiar about the woman. Something I can't quite put a finger on.

"Well, she didn't lie," Scarlett says. "I just wish she'd told me more. Every time I mentioned her past, she'd end up talking about something else."

"Could this woman have been a victim too? Maybe someone who helped her escape the ring and brought her to the river?"

"I mean, it's possible. Mama used to always talk about the river, said she made a lot of good memories here. When we helped Emily escape, Mama must've remembered enough from her childhood to feel comfortable taking us back here. After all, there are plenty of places to hide."

1986. Almost forty years and forty summers ago. Enough time for this woman to have grown old or passed away. And yet, she's the only link to Samantha's past.

I look at the photo again, hold the woman's gaze. The longer I stare, the more certain I am of this woman's identity, even if my stubbornness makes me not want to believe it.

It's Ms. Judy—I'm almost sure of it. But then how did she know Samantha, Scarlett's mom? Did she smuggle Samantha out of the human trafficking ring? Was she once involved with the ring herself?

Maybe Scarlett's right and I don't know Ms. Judy as well as I thought. Or maybe I'm overthinking this.

"Come on," I tell Scarlett, after rummaging through more of the boxes and coming up short, no sign of the book anywhere. All we have is a photograph—one that poses more questions.

Once we leave, the storm is nearly gone, soaking the swamp to the bone. Rain drips from the slick-black branches, drenching the sand, covering the floor of the boat.

The photo now stored away in my pocket, I climb aboard the skiff as Scarlett huddles back beneath the tarp.

"We can try again some other time," I say. "Come back when it's safe."

Scarlett's voice sounds from beneath the plastic. "I don't like this place. Why do you think Mama hid the book here?"

Dead River. Summer of '86.

What does it mean?

"I have no idea," I say.

Ms. Judy's words replay in my head. *Best to just leave it alone.*

At the landing, my phone buzzes inside my pocket. Once. Twice.

I fish it out, noticing the notifications onscreen, all within the last hour.

Two missed calls. They must just now be coming through.

I open the phone app, call the number back.

"Hello?" someone grumbles after the second ring. My heart skips. *Lynn.* "Clay? That you?"

I check the time onscreen. *9:52.* Almost an hour late for my shift.

"Yeah, it's me," I say, hoping she can't detect the nervous quiver in my voice.

How many times has this happened now? How many more chances is Lynn willing to give?

"Listen, I meant to call you earlier, but I lost service. I got caught up with something here at the river. Something bad's happened."

I gulp down a breath of air, nearly choking. Technically, it's not *not* a lie.

"I figured as much. Everything alright?"

Once again, her calm, considerate approach catches me off guard. "No, the police found another body, this time at Hidden Creek. Wouldn't let me pass. Tied me up with a lot of questions. It's not like I could leave."

The lies come out so effortless, so natural. Before this week, I can't remember another time I ever lied to my *boss*.

"That's the reason I called you," Lynn whispers, a hint of urgency to the words. "There's a detective here asking to see you."

A detective…Detective Conaughey? I roll my eyes at the thought of facing him again, answering his pointless questions. Haven't I told him enough?

"Stubby black beard? White button-up shirt? Smells of cigarettes?"

Lynn takes a second to answer. "No. Not at all. This one's different. Clean-cut, expensive suit, and official-looking. This man means business. He's more than a little upset that you haven't shown."

In the bow, Scarlett sits up, takes a look around the empty parking lot. She's probably wondering where she's going, what comes after this.

To be honest, I sure as hell don't know. After all, how long can we afford to keep up this ruse before the people from the ring quit looking for her, realizing it's a lost cause? How long before the police catch on?

It's for the best, I kept telling myself on the way back. It's not like Scarlett can stay at the river any longer. Not with the police a mile away, conducting their crime scene. They're bound to find her there before long.

If that happened, I doubt I'd ever see her again. I doubt I'd ever be able to find her.

But my promise links us together, keeps our lives intertwined.

No matter what happens, I won't leave her. Not like everyone else left me. She's my main priority now. More than Bart's and some nosy, plains-clothed detective.

Okay, *two* detectives. One who wants to find Scarlett, and the other who wants hell knows what.

With an edge of venom to my voice that I wouldn't have dared attempt a week ago, I say, "Tell him to wait. I'm busy."

Then I hang up.

28

HEARSAY

RAIN CATCHES US again before I finish hooking the boat to the truck. Fat, frigid drops striking my face, dripping from my cap.

"Hurry!" I say to Scarlett, who's holding the tarp above her head as a makeshift covering in the steady downpour.

This time, she doesn't hesitate.

Once I'm finished, I slide into the driver's seat and remove my soaked Under Armour cap—a birthday present from Dad—while Scarlett asks the inevitable. "Where are we going?"

Teeth chattering, I shift the truck in gear. "Home," I tell her. "We're going home."

Raindrops pelt the front window glass, partially obscuring the path ahead. If not for the exhaustive effort of the windshield wipers, thumping back and forth, back and forth, I wouldn't be able to see the road in front of me.

"And where might that be exactly?"

I sneak a glance in her direction. She's huddled low in the passenger seat, ducking whenever a car edges past. Yellow headlights and red taillights are the only visible indicators of another vehicle through the hazy rainstorm. "Somewhere safe," I say. "It's not far."

And then, before she can interject: "Listen, I have to go back to Bart's for something. I shouldn't be gone long, but in the meantime, you'll need to stay in my room. Promise you can do that?"

When she speaks this time, her voice sounds clearer, more certain, but maybe it's because the rain has let up, now no more than a faint trickle against the glass. "Yeah, I promise."

"Good."

"Clay?"

"Yeah?"

"Speed up. Storm's almost over. You drive like a kid who just got his permit."

I bite my lip, increase my speed to a comfortable fifty-five on the slick-wet pavement, and don't say another word.

I park the truck in the backyard, taking Scarlett's hand and leading her through the knee-high grass, up the three rickety wooden porch steps, and past the screen door. It bangs shut behind us before I can grab it.

"Up the stairs. First door on the right," I whisper into her ear.

We're halfway through the dining area when a familiar voice calls out from the next room. "Jason?"

Crap. Not now.

I grip Scarlett's hand tighter, practically yanking her in the direction of the stairs.

Just three more steps. Two. One—

"Jason? That you?"

At the sound of Grandpa's voice, Scarlett stiffens, stopping dead in her tracks. She tosses a quick glance over her shoulder at the exact moment he hobbles into the room, leaning against the doorframe and taking in the sight of us, dripping wet onto the tile floor.

I shove the rain-soaked hair back from my brow, letting go a sigh.

We've been caught.

"Yeah. It's me."

My hand drops from Scarlett's, but not before Grandpa notices. His eyebrows twitch. "Who's this?"

"She's just a friend. From school." I hope my cheeks aren't as red as they feel. "She offered to help me on some math homework. It's due tomorrow."

Fingers crossed he doesn't notice the calendar hanging on the dining room wall over my shoulder, the current date—June 23rd—outlined in red Sharpie. Over twenty-five days since school let out for the summer.

Beside me, Scarlett has gone still, and it's not until Grandpa utters a curt *Oh, I see* that I remember to breathe.

The words come easier now. "We'll be in my room if you need us."

But Grandpa ignores me, stepping so close I can smell the abrasive scent of Old Spice cologne and leather shoe polish. "What is your name, young lady? You sure do look familiar."

I will a peek at Scarlett, who's edged slowly back in the direction of where we came, eyes wide as if she's seen a ghost. "Umm, I don't—"

"Scarlett, come on." I grab her arm this time, gently pulling her along. "We have work to do."

"Hey, I know you." Grandpa clicks his tongue against the roof of his mouth, pointing a finger at her face. "Golly, you sure haven't changed a bit."

"Talk later. Bye."

We turn our backs on him, feet thumping up the stairs. Outside my room, Scarlett pauses. "Something you need to tell me, *Jason*?"

I roll my eyes. "It's a long story."

"Look who finally decided to show up." Lynn's voice is cold as ice when I finally arrive to Bart's a half hour after our call. But I don't pay her any mind, instead holding out a hand to the detective leaning against the counter.

"Clayton Thomas. So sorry to keep you waiting. I ran into some trouble back at the river."

Hopefully, Lynn didn't *really* tell him what I said.

His expression remains the same, somewhere between annoyed and tired. Like any other detective, dark bags bulge beneath his eyes, as if he didn't get much sleep the night before. His calloused hand grips my own. "Detective Keyes. Mind if we have a quick word?"

Curt and to-the-point. I imagine he does this all the time.

"I don't mind at all."

I follow Detective Keyes into the small hallway near the back of the store, past the restroom and into Lynn's office. My heart beats faster as he closes the door behind, motioning for me to sit.

What could he possibly want to know?

Detective Keyes leans against a corner of Lynn's desk, removing something from his pocket and holding it up for me to see. "Have you seen this girl?"

Even in the pale office lighting, I don't have any trouble at all recognizing the blond, almost yellow hair, green eyes, and the smatter of freckles across the bridge of the teen's nose. It's an older photo, one of Scarlett hunched over a giant sink, scrubbing a plate and sticking her tongue out at the camera, probably taken by one of her coworkers at that seafood joint in Panama City. Her spunk makes me curious to know who she might've been before, if maybe losing her mother stripped away all of that liveliness. It almost makes me wonder if it's the only documented picture of Scarlett the authorities have in their possession, besides her portraits in school yearbooks, which I doubt even exist; her mother most likely signed a form to exempt Scarlett from all photos. Still, she strikes me as a girl who wouldn't willingly be caught dead in the flash of a camera.

"What's this about?"

"Just answer my question, Mr. Thomas."

"No. I haven't seen her."

He puts the photo back in his pocket. My eyes lock onto a small grease stain on his tie. "According to her coworkers in Panama City, she hasn't shown up in over a week. But since she's eighteen, we can't officially declare her missing. We also haven't been able to get in touch with any living relative. One of her coworkers suspects she ran away, maybe came up here. Talked about some place down at the river where her mother used to stay. And, since this is the only store around, I can't help but wonder if you've seen her."

"Listen, I've already talked to a detective about this. Told him all I know."

Detective Keyes doesn't even flinch. "Yeah? And who might that be? When was this?"

"A few days ago. His name's Detective Conaughey. Said he worked for the Sheriff's Department."

The man arches an eyebrow, finally showing interest. "Conaughey, Conaughey," he mutters. "Sorry. Doesn't ring a bell."

"Here." I dig out the business card, hand it over. I'm surprised I've kept it this long instead of tossing it in the trash. "This has his contact info."

Detective Keyes eyes it for a moment, flips it over. Maybe it's a trick of the light, but it almost seems as though his cheeks have grown two shades lighter. "Where did he talk to you?"

"Here. At the store."

"And what did you tell him?"

"Said I'd let him know if I saw her around. Why? Did I say something wrong?"

"No, not at all," Detective Keyes says. "I've never heard of him, which is odd since we'd work in the same department."

His forehead creases as I consider what he's implying. It doesn't make any sense.

Any moment now, I expect him to pop off another question, but it's clear this new piece of information has caught him off guard. He seems genuine. I doubt he'd lie about a fellow associate.

I stand from the chair. "If I run into the girl or happen to see her by any chance, I'll let somebody at your department know."

The detective stares at the card a second more before noticing me backing in the direction of the door. "Yes, please do. I left one of these with your boss. You know, just in case."

Once we're back in the front of the shop, the bell clanking against the door in Detective Keyes's wake, Lynn asks, "What happened back there? Looks like he saw a ghost."

"Not much. He's looking for a missing girl. Wanted to know if I'd seen her somewhere around town or here in the store."

I don't dare mention the real reason he left in such a hurry. To be fair, I'm still not sure how I feel about the detective's reaction. Why would Detective Conaughey lie about where he worked? And why had Detective Keyes never heard of him?

"That's what I figured," Lynn says, staring out the glass doors into the parking lot, chewing on a hangnail. "But something about it seemed odd. The way you've been acting lately, showing up late, and then some detective comes in looking for you...something about it doesn't feel right."

Lynn reaches for a box of Cheez-Its behind the register, cramming a hand inside and popping several crackers into her mouth. "And don't worry," she says, between mouthfuls. "I'm not mad at you. Not this time. Besides, it's your paycheck, not mine."

I think back to our phone call earlier. *There's a detective here asking to see you.*

"I thought he was here to ask me about the body."

"Guess not," she says, "even though it *is* already all over Facebook."

"What are they saying?"

"Not much. Just a bunch of hearsay. You know, the same old mess. But it does make me worry for that girl. You swear you haven't seen her out there in the swamp?"

"No. Of course I haven't."

Scarlett's words replay in my head: *You're a terrible liar.*

"Why? Have you?"

Lynn closes the box, wiping the crumbs off her hands. "Nope. I hope I'd remember something like that. And I hope she's not caught up in it, I really do. Prostitution is no world for a girl that young to be involved in."

Something Lynn grumbled once while skimming the front page of *The River Gazette* comes to mind—something about a sex-ring bust further south. *They say Highway 98 stretching from Pensacola to Panama City is just one long road for hookers. Nasty, skanky women who'll sleep with anything and anybody for a little cash.*

"It's no world for any girl," I say. "You think that's what she is...a prostitute? You think that's what all those girls were?"

"Think about it, Clay. All the cases are too similar for it to be anything else. I bet you it's all the same man, like a new Ted Bundy. Finds himself the right type and then he's on to the next."

"But I thought you said that was all a bunch of hearsay."

"Yeah, well…the hearsay might be right."

"I think you need to stay off Facebook, Lynn. It's not good for the mind."

Lynn doesn't miss a beat. "And I think you need to get your butt to work on time. It's not good for business."

I chuckle to myself. At least Lynn hasn't lost her spunk.

"And Clay?" she asks before I can head to my corner of the store. "You might think you're fooling me, and you might have let that detective off the hook, but I know something's up. A week ago you come in here asking away about a dead body. And now, only days later, they've found another one. I think you know something you're not telling."

"I promise, Lynn. It's nothing but a coincidence."

I turn away before I can see her reaction or catch another one of her sly remarks.

A few little screw-ups and she's all on my case.

From here on out, I need to keep my mouth shut, before my lies catch up with me.

29

IN THE DARK

SCARLETT'S SITTING ON my bed when I return to the house an hour later, a leather-bound photo album splayed across her lap. Lynn gave me the rest of the day off, even though I could tell she thought better of it. Though, I guess in her mind, it's not every day you're questioned by a detective about a missing girl.

Now, Scarlett's hair is held in place by a towel, and based on the running exhaust fan and the light glowing from the underside of my bathroom door, I assume she's not long finished from a shower. She's changed into a pair of sweats—baggy, of course—and a vintage T-shirt of some rock band whose prime time was in the early 90s.

"You didn't tell me about your dad," Scarlett says, removing what looks like a cream-colored brochure from the center of the photo album, tucked inside a plastic sleeve.

Instantly, I know what she's found, and just as sudden, my heart sinks.

It's Dad's obituary.

"Put it back," I say, my voice soft.

"You lied to me, Clay," she whispers. The realization of those five words settles deep within my gut like heavy stones.

I imagine she won't believe a word I say. After all, why should she trust me? If she thinks I lied to her about Dad, what else might she think I've been dishonest about?

An even worse question—one that makes my chest tighten and my breath hitch—settles on my conscience, makes me take a step back: is the truth enough to make her leave?

I lick my lips, forcing out a lousy, "I can explain..."

Scarlett puts the obituary back where it came from, but not before I catch a glimpse of the photo on the front cover—a younger version of Dad with his fishing cap on backwards and a can of Mountain Dew in hand, caught mid-laugh.

I remember that day. We hadn't caught anything—at least, nothing substantial enough to count—but that didn't stop Dad from trying anyway, hoping for a miracle.

Soon enough, he'd gotten a satisfying tug on the end of his line—*I've got a nice sized one,* he'd muttered, a fresh sheen of sweat gleaming along his forehead as he reeled in his catch—but instead of a channel cat, it was some old man's leather boot, probably decades old.

I'd taken that photo. I'd even turned it in to the funeral home director myself. I'd picked out his casket. I'd chosen the hymns to sing in-between speakers and even tallied a list of pallbearers' names, which Dad whispered in my ear from his hospital bed.

It seemed I'd done everything, just like always.

In return, all I'd received were dozens of awkward, cologne-heavy hugs, elbow squeezes, pitied looks, and disconcerting words from a pastor who made Dad sound like a saint—careful and poised and genuine to a fault, when in fact, that was no description of the man I'd known all my life.

Dad was caring and optimistic, with a certain rawness to his words, but he was no saint. He was human, just like the rest of us. A man who did all he could for me and Grandpa and then abandoned us when we needed him most. One who made promises he couldn't keep and said things that made more sense as lies.

This was meant to happen to us, Clay. I know you may not understand it now, but these moments must come and go. They make us stronger. They help us heal.

But I'm no stronger than the day he left; than the day Mom walked right out of our lives.

If anything, both times only made me lonelier, more desperate, and so bitter that some mornings I didn't even want to crawl out of bed.

"There's something else," Scarlett says, snapping me from my thoughts. "Something I think you should see." She reaches for a quart-sized Ziploc bag on the bed beside her—something I didn't notice before with my distraction with the obituary. "It's about your mother. I'm guessing you didn't know anything about these, did you?"

The plastic bag crinkles in her hands as she holds it out to me, a clutter of envelopes packed inside.

"Where did you find—"

"Just take it, Clay."

I inhale a deep breath, the mere mention of my mother bringing back every painful memory.

Those blinding red heels, click-clacking down the walk and the front door closing behind her. Standing on tiptoe, watching from a crack in the blinds as she loaded the boxes into her trunk, before slamming it shut, yanking open the driver's side door, and driving like hell down the street.

In a way, it's as if my mother died years ago. Here one day, gone the next.

But I have to remind myself that it was her decision, after all, to leave me and Dad. In my mind, she planned it all out, saw no other option.

Over the years, there have been no letters. No birthday cards or Christmas presents. Not even one phone call.

I don't know where she ended up or whose ring she wears now or what she even looks like. Honestly, I've been in the dark so long about everything that encompasses my mother that I don't want to understand her; don't want to consider why she never bothered to reach out to me again or call every now and then just to hear my voice.

She could be dead for all I know.

She could be a missing woman whose picture is plastered across some other town's storefronts and telephone poles or a prisoner caught in the slave trade.

She could be anywhere and anyone.

And now Scarlett holds the answer in her hand, urging me to look, to finally know.

Grudgingly, I accept, opening the bag and stuffing a hand inside until my fingers brush against paper.

Eleven letters. One for every year she's been gone.

Written and signed in her elegant cursive. Addressed to me.

I read a few sentences from the first one until my lungs constrict and the back of my throat burns, and I decide I've seen enough.

Dear Clay, my little boy. I miss you so, so much. I think about you every day. Your smile. Your infectious laugh. I hope your dad is treating you well. I hope he whispers I love you *for me every night before bed...*

"Where did you find this?"

Scarlett tugs on the end of her sock, face flushing red with guilt. "Down the stairs, first door on the left. I'm guessing it was your dad's room. Found them in a sock drawer."

Of course. Having me gone was the perfect opportunity for her to snoop around behind my back. As if, after everything I've done for her, I'm the one to be wary of, the boy with a secret life, a secret past.

To her, maybe that's how it looks.

"I told you to stay put. Why couldn't you just listen?"

"Because I got suspicious, Clay," she says. "After your grandpa called you by a different name, I couldn't help but feel like you weren't telling me something. And then I found that obituary and got curious. I needed to know what else you might be keeping from me. Besides, I remember you saying something about your mother leaving you as a kid, and I started to wonder if even that was a lie. When I found the letters, some part of me knew your dad never showed them to you...*if* what you said before was true." She takes a breath, and I feel her gaze on the side of my face as I skim the lines of each letter—a way to distract myself from the more pressing issue that Scarlett knows more than I ever wanted her to. "Do you miss her?" she asks a second later.

The answer should be a given. It shouldn't require this much thought. Before now, I would've shaken my head and told her *no*.

But *this*. This changes things. Dad kept this from me. All this time, Mom cared enough to put pen to paper and, in return, Dad buried the evidence in the bottom of a sock drawer.

If she went to all that effort, how many of her calls have I missed over the years? How many cards did Dad intercept and make sure I never saw?

Did he want to erase her from my mind completely?

Did he really want me to forget my own mother?

"Somehow, I do," I finally answer. Even if she wasn't around for most of my life, I can't help but think that things would have been a whole lot easier for all of us. Mom was our constant, the piece that held us together. Without her, we were a Jenga tower destined to fall.

All this time, I thought she couldn't care less about me. About *us*.

Turns out I couldn't have been more wrong.

Still, Scarlett's not convinced. "Why would your dad keep this from you?"

"He wanted to protect me," I say, the only truth I can fathom. "I guess he knew that if I kept thinking of her, she'd only hold me back and make me feel sorry for myself. But that's no excuse for what he did."

"I'm sorry, Clay. I just wanted you to know."

"I'm glad someone did. And I'm sorry, too. I shouldn't have lied. I just didn't want you to think less of me. To feel *bad* for me."

"Do you honestly think after everything I told you about my life that I would've held that fact against you?"

"No," I say. "I know you wouldn't have."

"We all have things we don't anyone else to know. It's human nature, natural instinct even, to keep it to ourselves. But it's better to get those things off your chest instead of keeping them in. No good comes from silence."

I let go a deep breath, placing everything back in the plastic bag and sealing it closed. "No one's ever bothered to hear it," I tell her.

"Well, I'm listening. I'd like to think you can trust me."

Before I can respond, Scarlett's stomach emits a low, rumbling sound. It's the perfect distraction.

"Come on," I say, tossing the bag of envelopes onto the bed and motioning for her to follow. "Let's see what Grandpa's got ready for dinner."

Scarlett stops me on the stairs, grips the bony part of my elbow until I face her. Just like that day on the dock, I can tell by the firm set of her lips that something's bothering her.

"What's wrong?"

"You sure about this?" she says, casting a cautious look down the remaining steps to the ground floor.

"Remember. You're just a friend...from school. And we have *a lot* of math homework."

"No, that's not what I meant." She lets me go, pressing her back against the wall, those long eyelashes fluttering open and closed, mouth agape, as if she's second guessing whether to tell me or not. "It's not safe for you if I stay here," she finally says, arms crossed like her mind's already made up.

"Looks like you don't have much of a choice. You're much better off here than somewhere on your own—"

"Yeah? Then how much longer do you expect to keep this up?"

I shrug. Honestly, I haven't thought much more about it. To me, it doesn't matter how long she stays here as long as she's out of harm's way. "We'll think of something," I say. "In the meantime, you need to lie low. Stay in my room, watch some TV, play a video game. I don't care. Eventually, they'll find whoever did this and we can think about what to do then."

"You don't get it," she mumbles, brushing her way past. "But you'll see. Can't say I didn't try and warn you."

"What's that supposed to mean?" I say to her back, but she's already down the stairs and around the corner, leaving yet another question unanswered in her wake.

I pile my plate with a heaping scoop of field peas, cream corn, and a slab of ribeye steak, fresh from the grill.

Sometimes, Grandpa still finds a way to surprise me, and this is one of them. He's cooking like he's supposed to, like old times, without me having to remind him of the obligation.

At the table—Scarlett beside me, Grandpa on the opposite side—we bow our heads and say grace. I will a quick peek at Scarlett as Grandpa babbles on and on, praying for safety and protection and Jason to do well on his math.

She meets my gaze before I can turn away, blushing red whenever Grandpa fumbles with her name—"I thank you for Sara or Sabrina or whoever Jason's friend is with us today"—and I try to hold back a snort of laughter.

Once Grandpa finishes the prayer after what feels like twenty minutes of holding our breath and trying not to snicker, we dig in, utensils scraping and cutting across our plates, drowning out the sound of our awkward silence.

"Hope you kids enjoy yourselves," Grandpa says a minute later, scooping up a spoonful of corn. "The women always enjoyed my cooking, especially my peas."

We'll see about that, I think, stuffing a heap of warm, salty field peas into my mouth. But instead of biting into something soft and mushy as expected, my back molars grind down on something hard and metallic, making me nearly spit out my mouthful of food.

Teeth throbbing in pain, I use two fingers to pull out an object about as big around as a coke tab, now covered in spit and remnants of mushed-up peas. "Grandpa, what did you put in these?"

"Oh," Grandpa says, setting down his utensils, "it must be your lucky day! Mama always used to put a penny in the peas on New Year's. Said it brought good luck."

I rest my head in my hands, letting out a groan. "But it's June, not January!"

Grandpa winks. "Exactly."

Out of the corner of my eye, I notice Scarlett biting back a grin, dragging her fork tines through her own clump of peas, searching for any flash of metal. Clearly, I didn't warn her about Grandpa's culinary skills.

Not a second later, a timer chimes from the stove.

"Dessert's ready," Grandpa says. But instead of getting up to go check on it himself, he stares right at Scarlett. I think about nudging her foot beneath the table to see if she notices but quickly decide against it.

"I'll get it," I say, standing from my chair just as Grandpa lets something slip under his breath.

I don't exactly understand all he says, but I do catch one word on my way to the stove, and it almost sounds like *Samantha*.

That night, I make Scarlett sleep in my bed, much against her protests, while I take the hard floor and a moth-eaten blanket from my closet. For now, at least, it'll have to do.

It takes everything within me not to ask about Grandpa and whether or not she heard the name he'd grumbled between bites of steak. Guessing on her silence on the manner, I assume she hadn't.

Now, a couple hours after dinner, I lie awake from my spot on the floor, listening to the drone of the fan above and trying to ignore the desire rippling through my veins, the dull ache in my chest that won't go away.

My thoughts revolve around one thing and one thing only, humming louder the instant I close my eyes and try to sleep. Only one thing will silence it, and my heart's racing way too fast for any amount of shut-eye, my hands trembling at the thought of what I'm about to do.

Now that she's here, it's easier to make sense of these feelings, but much more difficult to make them leave.

Scarlett stirs awake in my sheets, cracking an eye open and noticing me watching her.

For once, I don't look away.

In the dark, I can still make out the dimple that dents the side of her face whenever she smiles a certain way, making that warm and fluttery feeling return to my chest.

"Clay?" she mouths. "What are you doing?"

As if snapping from a hallucination, I look away, realizing my mistake.

Cheeks burning, I mumble, "Nothing. It's nothing."

"Come here," she says, patting the spot beside her as she rises to a sitting position, sheets bunched up to her chin. "I can't sleep. Rather just talk if that's okay."

Slowly, I sit on the edge of the bed, inches away from her now. I can't help but feel like I'm crossing some unspoken boundary, the thoughts inside my head tearing down the wall we've kept up for over a week.

My trembling fingers dig into the side of the mattress. "Can I tell you something?"

"Please," she snorts, edging closer. "I already know."

And then her lips press against mine.

The next few moments unravel like a dream. My hands beneath her shirt, pulling it over her head. The bedspread, cool against my bare skin, the mattress giving in, softer than I remember.

Her lips find my ear. "This isn't real," she whispers.

My eyes snap open and I'm back…back to my uncomfortable spot on the floor, tangled in the moth-eaten blanket, the fan whirring above, and the dulcet sounds of Scarlett's snoring drifting down to me.

A dream, I tell myself, crashing back to reality, vividly remembering the feel of my hands running up and down her spine and her lips pressing against my neck only moments before.

It was only a dream.

30

SMOKE

I **N THE MORNING,** I leave my phone and a number for Scarlett to call in case of an emergency on the nightstand beside my bed, heading off to Bart's.

Each time, leaving her becomes a little more difficult, but now everything within me desires to stay. Maybe it's a result of my dream from the night before or the fact that Grandpa is just as liable to stumble across her and call the cops.

I push away any other alternative from my mind, trying not to think of the shotgun beside Grandpa's armchair and the thought of him aiming it at someone as young as Scarlett.

As long as she remains in my room, everything should be fine.

"I have a message for you," Lynn says the moment I push through the glass doors, skimping on a proper welcome. She motions to the handheld phone beside the register.

"From who?" I ask, even though I already know.

Lynn rolls her eyes. "Ms. Judy. Who else?"

As I'm punching in the number, Lynn plops down on a barstool behind the counter and blows out a sigh. "The old gal seemed a little frazzled. Said it was important but wouldn't tell me nothing. Just insisted you call back soon as possible."

"Weird," I mumble.

In all my years of returning her calls, she's never sounded as urgent as when she picks up on the third ring, cutting straight to the chase. "Clay," Ms. Judy breathes. "I need you to come by whenever you get the chance. I know you're busy but there's something I've got to tell you."

Lynn's watching me. Picking up a pen and pretending to write something on the back of her hand, looking away the moment I catch her staring.

I press the phone tighter against my cheek, lowering my voice. "You can't tell me now?"

"No, not over the phone. I need to see you in person, before I change my mind."

"Okay. I'll stop by right after work." I think of Scarlett, hiding out in my room, and add, "But I can't stay long."

From somewhere in the background, I make out the chime of a doorbell. Once. Twice. "Alright," she exhales. "See you then. I've got to go. Someone's at the door."

She ends the call before I can tell her bye.

Lynn clicks the pen a few times before moving it to her mouth and sucking on the tip like a lit cigarette. "What'd she say?"

"Just wants to talk. Sounded like it was important."

I place the phone back in its cradle, wishing Lynn's boredom didn't cause her to be so nosy. "Important? What could be more important for an old woman other than crossword puzzles and reruns of *Golden Girls*?"

For once, I tell her the truth. "I have no idea."

Less than three hours later, I'm walking up Ms. Judy's gravel drive to the front porch, where I can usually find her sipping a can of Diet Coke and shouting something to me in greeting.

With every step I'm met with silence. With every step the more anxious I become, remembering her words: *There's something I've got to tell you.*

My fist raps against the wooden door.

"Ms. Judy?"

Nothing.

Usually, even if she doesn't know to expect me, I can discern her shadow though the closest window, outlined by the warm lamplight from the living room, and I can hear the creak of her steps across the ancient wooden floorboards to the front door.

Today, there is no shadow or dark outline of a figure through the glass. No distinguishable steps.

Hairs rise on the nape of my neck, just as they always do when something doesn't feel right. Just like now.

I've got to go. Someone's at the door.

I try the doorbell, wincing at the shrieking chime from within, seeming to increase in pitch the longer it echoes on, like a smoke detector in need of new batteries.

Once again, there is only silence.

I look back over my shoulder, spotting her silver Buick parked in the drive.

If her car's still here, then there's no way she isn't home.

With this in mind, I push back my concern long enough to reach for the doorknob and twist my way inside, into the quiet, shadowed house.

The smell strikes me first.

Nauseating and smoky, like something's been cooked far too long. Bypassing the living room, I head straight for the kitchen, easy enough to find at the end of a short hallway, the burning smell growing stronger with every step, stinging my eyes and nostrils.

Smoke curls from beneath the silver lid of a smoldering pot on the stovetop. Intuition kicking in, I lift the lid, waving a hand in front of my face to combat the pungent scent of burnt peas, speckled brown and black in the bottom of the pot.

The back of my throat burns as I grab the silver handle and move the pot off the red-hot eye, pressing the back of my hand across my mouth to keep from gagging.

Out of the corner of my eye, and through the gray haze now lingering in the air, I spot someone crumpled on the floor in a tangle of limbs several feet away.

Unmoving. Unconscious.

My vision blurs and I grip the edge of the counter to right myself.

"Ms. Judy?"

But she doesn't speak.

Something red covers the lenses of her glasses, both eyes staring right through me.

Lifeless. Dead.

I take a trembling step forward, almost slipping in a pool of blood.

Blood…blood everywhere.

Covering the floor, the walls, and gleaming wet from a slit in her throat.

"No," I manage to force out. "You have to get up…*get up*…"

I grab her arm, give it a soft tug, but it falls limp to her side like something rubber.

My breath catches, and for a moment, I don't breathe. "Ms. Judy…"

I barely make it to the sink before the vomit races up my throat, burning raw and hot from my mouth, over my chin, and coating the unwashed dishes and silverware within in a gritty, orange sludge.

Realization washes over me.

Someone was here. In this very spot.

The same person who killed her.

Blinking away the sting in my eyes, I snatch the closest phone from its mount on the wall, plastic cord and all, and dial 911.

31

SAMANTHA

AFTER THE COPS arrive, followed by a screeching ambulance and fire truck, I'm escorted to Ms. Judy's front porch, where a young female investigator asks me several questions. I try to answer as best as possible, even if all I can picture is the sight of the bloody kitchen floor and Ms. Judy's crumpled body whenever I close my eyes, distracted by the shuffle of EMTs and cops hurrying in and out whenever I try to concentrate on the woman's words.

What's your relationship with Ms. Jones?

Did you say the door was unlocked when you arrived?

Did you notice anything strange?

My voice sounds hollow and weak as I speak, and I hardly respond when she passes over her business card, writes down my number in a page in her notebook.

My head spins after she retreats into the house with the rest of her team. This can't be happening. This is a prank. This isn't real.

But then I think of what Scarlett said the night before: *It's not safe for you if I stay here.*

This couldn't have been a random robbery, a chance break-in. This had to have been connected. Not a coincidence. Scarlett warned me, and I didn't listen. Whoever is after her found us. Ms. Judy's death is a clear sign of that.

Grandpa's voice sounds in my mind this time. *The bad men are coming, Jason.*

Alone, in my truck, I finally give in to the pain and shock of the past hour, warm tears streaming down both cheeks. I swallow, trying to rid the acrid taste from my tongue.

Who would do something like this?

Who could hurt, much less kill, someone as kind and innocent as Ms. Judy?

Does it have anything to do with what she'd avoided to tell me that day in my boat?

That look she'd given Scarlett? The way she hesitated whenever I asked if the girl looked familiar? The casual slip-up of Scarlett's name?

Wiping the tears from my face, I head home, increasing my speed well over the required limit, thoughts and questions racing through my mind, failing to snap into place.

Cars and SUVs idle along Main Street, several customers clutching plastic cups outside the pizza joint, standing in a circle while their children hopscotch behind on the chalk-coated sidewalk, edging too close to the road. A woman flips the open sign to closed in the bakery's storefront, and the bright lights fade to dim in the antique store's glass windows.

As always, Delton is so sleepy it hurts, so mundane that for one passing second, I consider rolling down my window and shouting until my lungs ache, see if anyone cares enough to notice. Maybe if they'd heard that a woman had been murdered in her home only blocks away, they'd bother to watch out for their children and rush like hell to their cars.

By the six o'clock news, everyone will know, even if the police fail to release a name right away. One Facebook post by a nosy ass local who followed the sirens and the rumors will circulate. I can already imagine the comments.

Too many cop cars for her to have fallen again.

Poor thing. I hope she's okay. Praying.

Possible house fire? I thought I heard a fire truck.

In the meantime, I have to get home and make sure Scarlett's okay. I have to tell her I was wrong and that we're nowhere near as safe as I'd thought.

And that, once again, all of this is my fault.

"Scarlett?"

I bound up the stairs, adrenaline thrumming through my veins.

Three steps from my bedroom, I call out again. "Scarlett!"

No answer.

When the door peels open, I realize why.

The room is empty. The rumpled bed sheets are untucked from the corners, brushing against the carpet. My phone and note are in the same spot as before, on the nightstand beside the bed.

Beneath my words—*Bart's at 9. Be home this afternoon*—are four new ones, hurriedly written in black Sharpie marker at the bottom of the sticky note: *Thank you for everything.*

Realization washes over me at the same time a door slams downstairs.

Someone yells.

I'd know that voice anywhere.

"Grandpa?" I call out, taking the stairs two steps at a time.

I find him below, in the living room, staring straight ahead at the front door as if in a trance. Something long and black protrudes from his shoulder.

I blink and my vision sharpens.

"What are you doing with that gun?"

He turns, points the barrel at me, until I'm face to face with the end of the 12 gauge shotgun.

"Someone was in our house," he says, doe-eyed and trembling.

"It's okay. It was just Scarlett."

"Who?"

The gun still aimed at my face, I whisper, "Put it down, Grandpa. It's me. It's Jason."

After one long, tense second, he obeys, lowering the shotgun and casting another suspicious glance out the closest window overlooking the driveway.

Outside, an engine revs, breaking my attention from Grandpa and his loaded weapon to the key rack beside the front door.

My keys.

They're gone.

One second I'm bolting for the door, and the next I'm outside, feet pounding the paved drive as a cry rips from my throat, arms waving above my head. *"Stop!"*

Fury churning in my chest, I watch helplessly as my truck speeds down the street, tires screeching on asphalt. The trailer holding the Jon boat swings right and left, back and forth, in its wake.

She took my truck, I think, my stomach folding into itself.

I watch as it rounds the corner, slipping from sight.

"I'm calling the police," Grandpa grunts from behind.

From the open doorway, I notice him watching, waiting for me to respond.

"No." I force down a breath long enough to grit out the words. "Please. Don't."

Grandpa's lips pinch into a thin line. "She broke into our house!"

"I know how it looks. I know you're confused," I say, holding up a hand. "But you can't call the police."

I take a step forward, startling him enough to raise the gun in my direction, then lowering it once he comes to his senses. "Just tell me what I need to do."

"I know where she's going," I say. "I need to follow her."

"Jason, that's not safe."

Ignoring him, I trace my steps back to the door. "I need a boat. Need to get to the river."

But before I can cross the threshold, snatching another pair of keys from the rack beside the door, Grandpa blocks my path, shields my entrance. "I don't think so."

"Grandpa!" I practically scream. "I. Don't. Have. Time! Someone's after her...after *us*...and if I don't stop her in time, then it'll all be my fault!"

Grandpa blinks. "Who's after you, Jason?"

"The bad men! The same people who killed Scarlett's mother. Samantha. Her name was Samantha. Does that sound familiar?"

I need him to move. I need him to snap out of it for once. The more time that passes only widens the gap for Scarlett to gather the rest of her things, retrieve her gun, and disappear for good.

"The river," I tell him, and something shifts behind his eyes, stare going glassy.

Gun falling to his side, he says, "Jason. You remember the night we found that little girl at the river?"

I bite my lip. Here we go again. Another story. Another moment wasted. Even though it's the worst possible time, I nod and say, "Yeah. I do."

What in the world does this have to do with Samantha?

And then I know.

"The little girl," I whisper. "Do you know who she was?"

"Of course," he says, looking over my shoulder now, focused on nothing in particular. I daresay he's lost in the past, caught in a distant memory. Back at Mile Lake that night, the little girl's screams piercing the night air. "Her name was Samantha."

32

INTUITION

ONCE I'VE RETRIEVED my phone and an old key chain from the rack by the front door, I focus my attention on Grandpa's '98 Chevy Silverado parked in the knee-high grass around the back of the house. My gaze travels along its side, the once fiery-red tint faded by years of sun and dust. I can't even remember the last time it left the yard.

Inside, the smell of the cracked vinyl seats and stained carpet conjures a memory.

I'm propped on my mother's lap in the backseat, her hands tucked beneath both of my armpits, bouncing me up and down on her knee, as she whisper-sung in my ear all the while. Dad in the passenger seat, humming along to some John Mellencamp song blasting from the speakers, while Grandpa remained focused and alert behind the wheel, talking around a mouthful of wintergreen snuff.

"Ain't got nothing on George Strait," he said.

Five years old, and I can still recall the time when my entire world existed in that truck, before Mom left and Dad stopped listening to the radio, the car rides strangely silent those following months; before Grandpa started using the car wash on the south side of town that shut down the year I was born, the lot vacant and crawling with vines, inserting one too many coins in the rusted slot box.

Now, I pull the seat belt across my lap, lock it into place, and insert the keys into the ignition, holding my breath as the truck sputters and gasps amid a cough of black smoke.

After a few seconds, the truck hums to life, and I press down too fast on the accelerator, lurching me forward in my seat, the belt taut against my chest.

I pretend not to notice Grandpa standing beneath the branches of a large oak tree in the backyard, probably watching me the entire time it took to start the engine. Any other time, I'd probably give more thought about telling him to get inside and lock the doors, given a killer on the prowl.

Anything other than Scarlett and the memory of Ms. Judy's body on the kitchen floor is the farthest thing from my mind. For one fleeting moment, I consider his revelation about Scarlett's mother and the irony that I'd found Scarlett just as Grandpa had found Samantha all those years before; the irony that is the sound of John Mellencamp's voice echoing through radio static all these years later.

Intuition kicks in about a mile from my house, nothing but the blur of pine trees and the occasional white-brick house appearing through window glass, and I pull my phone from my pocket. My gaze flicking back and forth between the screen and the narrow stretch of road ahead, I search for Detective Keyes' number, only to realize that I never got around to saving it in my phone. Instead, I locate Detective Conaughey's number. Deep down, some part of me knew I'd eventually need it. He's not my first choice, but at this point I can't afford to be picky.

"Hello?" a husky voice says after the second ring.

"I'm ready to talk."

"Who is this?"

"Clay. The guy from Bart's."

A second of pause. "Clay. That's right. What can I help you with?"

The words fly from my lips. "It's about that girl you're looking for."

"Yeah? What about her?"

"I know where she is. But I'll only tell you under one condition."

He doesn't say anything right away, almost as if the news catches him off guard. I can almost picture him sitting behind his desk, reaching for a pen, the ballpoint hovering over a blank sheet of paper. "What kind of condition?"

I take a shallow breath and let the words go in a rush. "I want you to forget everything you've heard. This girl's in trouble, detective. I don't know what you think happened between her and her father, but it's not true. It's not what you think. She's told me all kinds of things…*bad* things…about her past. How her mother got caught up in something dangerous and they've both been on the run for years. How they fled to the river to escape the men who are hunting them. I can show you where she is, but only if you keep her safe, find someplace for her to stay. I want to help her, I really do, but it's cost me too much already, and I just can't do it anymore. Can you promise you'll help? Can you promise you'll find the people who are after her?"

I almost swear he pauses for a reason, either to take notes on the information I provided or to think things through. "Of course," he says, after a moment. "Where can I meet you?"

"I'm headed to the river," I say, relief flooding through me at the detective's cooperation. After all, Scarlett means too much for me to not do the right thing, even if that does mean breaking our promise. Even if that does mean her safety over her life, before Ms. Judy's killer finds her next. "Give me ten minutes. If it's any later, I'll let you know."

"Thanks, Clay. And don't worry about this. I believe you, and of course I'm willing to help. Any information on Scarlett's whereabouts is vital in order to…"

His voice fades away, akin to static on the other end of the line, as realization takes hold, clenching my lungs in its icy cold grip.

Scarlett. That's what he said.

But how in the world would he know something like that if the missing person's report he'd shown me that day at Bart's was for a Danielle Brown?

"Hold up. Can you repeat that?"

This time, there is no hesitation in his response. "I'll see you at the river, Clay."

And then the line goes dead.

Lynn's house sits at the end of a dirt road on the north side of town, where one of the many creeks from the river cuts through her backyard, the glistening water offering a new route to intercept Scarlett.

Prior to now, stirring up dust as sticks snap beneath my tires in the mile-long drive, I've stopped by several times to complete a quick errand for Lynn or pick up a package delivered to her house instead of Bart's. I've also been by enough to know where she keeps her bass boat at the end of a wooden dock, parked beneath a small boat shed in order to keep the floors and insides from filling up with rain.

I park only feet away from the tranquil creek, its surface slick and black. The soles of my tennis shoes slap along the wooden planks as a yell sounds from behind, in the direction of the house, making me slide to a halt. "What do you think you're doing?"

Not even looking up, I step into the boat, notice the key already inserted into the ignition. The metal turns in my hand, motor rumbling to life.

The planks shudder as someone races along them, straight for me.

Her smoker's voice cuts like a knife. "Clay? What the—"

"I need your boat! Someone stole mine. I have to hurry."

Lynn stops at the edge, hands on her hips. "You need me to call the police?"

I meet her eyes, expecting steel or anger behind them. Instead, all I spot are wrinkles of worry etched in the lines of her face, concern in her wide-eyed stare.

"Already did," I answer back.

"I don't expect you're going to tell me who's behind this..."

"Lynn," I say, an edge to my voice. "I don't have time."

"Then go," she says, with a flick of her wrist. "But if this has anything to do with why you've been acting so strange lately, then I expect answers when you get back."

"I promise I'll tell you everything."

She nods, crossing her arms. "Alright. But be careful. I mean it."

I shift the tiller forward, the vessel sliding out from beneath the shed and into the sun, sending up a spray of water.

As the dock fades from view, I swear I hear Lynn screaming one last time for me to *be careful*.

But maybe it's just the wind.

33

FEAR

THE CREEK LEADS to the straightaway, a vital shortcut less than a mile from Scarlett's houseboat through the trees and river swamp. Halfway there, my phone vibrates against my thigh, but I don't have to look to know who it might be.

Conaughey, probably wondering why I haven't bothered to call back. But I don't have to, now that I know the truth. Now, it all makes sense why Detective Keyes had never heard of Conaughey before, and why Keyes appeared so flustered when I told him about being questioned by another cop on Scarlett's whereabouts only days before. Maybe Keyes suspected Conaughey was a fake before we even left Lynn's office. Maybe he called the number listed at the bottom of Conaughey's deceptive business card, knowing in his gut that something wasn't right about the whole thing. Then again, maybe Conaughey just as easily led him on, feeding Keyes more or less the same lies to keep the police from breathing down his neck.

Either way, I've failed. I even let my secret slip to Conaughey, hinting at Scarlett's location—quite possibly my most foolish deed since finding Samantha and refusing to tell anyone, specifically those who could've helped prevent another body from being dumped in the same condition, in the same place.

Then I'm reminded of that statistic—thirty-three bodies discarded on the riverbank over the years. Seventy percent of them women. Ninety percent of their cases unsolved.

Going to the police might not have done anything but clear my conscience.

Rounding the final bend of Lost Lake, I notice the sun glinting off aluminum in a spot along the shore of palmettos.

It's my boat—the same one Scarlett stole when she raced away in my truck, her only escape back to this place.

But this time, it appears that she's not alone.

That much becomes clear the moment I lock eyes with the bearded man standing in the middle of a white center-console boat, idling several feet away from the end of the floating dock, something gripped in his hand. Realization ripples through me, and I recall the metallic clang of the shots striking the boat that day and Scarlett's shrill screams, causing my heart to pulse faster, louder.

It's the same boat that followed us four days ago, and the same man who fired his gun in our direction, bullets missing us by inches.

A thick lump of fear forms in my throat. When I swallow, the lump tightens, like a noose.

Powering off my engine, my skiff crawls to a stop beside the center-console boat.

"Conaughey," I say, somehow finding my voice. Several inches separate us now. "What have you done with Scarlett?"

"Please," he snorts. Not a second later, his lips curl back into a sick smirk. "Call me detective."

Then I notice the silver pistol aimed on my chest.

34

GUNSHOT

DON'T BREATHE FOR what feels like hours, all the possible worst-case scenarios racing through my mind, none of them good.

Conaughey must've followed Scarlett here from the landing, recognizing my truck. After she parked and tried to slip undetected down the river, and before she could escape inside her houseboat, I imagine he fired several shots and watched her crumple. Maybe Conaughey even threw Scarlett's body in the palmettos or inside his boat, waiting for me to arrive so he could do the same.

"I'm guessing you've heard about the old woman," he says, snapping me from my grim thoughts. "It was a foolish decision on her part to let me in, but tell someone you're a cop and flash a fake badge in their face and they'll believe anything you have to say."

"She was harmless." The lump in my throat is now so taut I can hardly force down a breath, heart thumping at the possibility of how close I am to meeting the same fate.

"You honestly think I could risk it?" He edges several steps closer, the gun never once wavering in his approach. "This is your fault. Not mine. If you hadn't found that camera, then it's highly likely she'd still be alive right now."

"It wasn't like that. She didn't mean to," I almost scream, but now I'm not so sure if that's even scratching the surface of the truth at all.

Why had Ms. Judy gotten rid of that camera?

Why had she acted so secretive after?

What you don't know can't hurt you, son, she said. *Best to just leave it alone.*

"You watched us that day," I say, the only possible explanation for how he would know Ms. Judy threw his game camera in the river.

"Damn right I did," Conaughey snorts. "If you think that was the only camera I had out there, you're a bigger dumb ass than I thought. Entire swamp's full of 'em. It was only a matter of time before I found Scarlett's hideout anyway. Thankfully, you helped me out with that."

"But finding some hidden game camera isn't reason enough to break into a woman's house and murder her."

He shrugs. "You're right. I have a habit of not telling the whole truth— my bad. The truth is this: a couple days back, I saw this car parked real close to the boat landing. Struck me as sort of strange, so I went over and introduced myself. Behind the wheel was this old woman; I recognized her from the game camera. So I showed her Scarlett's picture, told her to be on the look-out...you know, the whole run-down. But I could tell there was something off about her. She hesitated too long before answering, kind of like she knew something. Thought: I can't risk it. Old gal acts like she knows too much."

He smiles at me. I don't smile back.

"Where's Scarlett?" I ask again.

Conaughey doesn't answer—he just continues to smile and hold my icy glare.

"If you're going to shoot me, then go ahead. But leave Scarlett alone. She's been through enough."

"Who's to say I haven't already..." He mimes a gun to his head with his thumb and pointer finger. "Well, you know."

Both of us turn at the squeal of rusty door hinges from the houseboat behind. A blond head pokes out first.

"Don't listen to him, Clay."

It's Scarlett.

"Oh my God," I breathe. The knot in my throat loosens. "You're okay."

"Of course I am," she says, her jaw clenched and her eyes trained on Conaughey's silver pistol as she steps out from the doorway. "Put down the gun and let him go."

My attention snaps back to Conaughey, gaze snagging on his knuckles tightening around the hilt of his weapon.

"Oh, so now you want to talk." He rolls his eyes, then his ice-cold gaze meets mine. "Bet she didn't tell you who I was."

Scarlett balls her fists. "That's enough."

"Bet she didn't tell you I'm her father."

"Enough!" As the word leaves Scarlett's lips, a shiver creeps down my spine. I can't tell what's worse—Scarlett's palpable anger, like a bomb ready to diffuse any given moment, or Conaughey's smirk, which makes me wish I was holding the gun myself.

"That's right," he says, raising his head a little higher, daring to flash a yellow-toothed smile. "Met her mother at a bar, fell in love, and then, a year later, Scarlett was born. My little girl. My whole world."

"I mean nothing to you," Scarlett practically spits, eyes narrowing.

Conaughey goes on. "It took a few years, but once her mother found out what I *really* did for a living, and I found out how she was undermining my operation, she took our daughter and fled like the coward she was. But twelve years later, here we are. And to think all it took was a phone call from Emily to one of the other girls in the ring for me to know where to find my family." His yellow-toothed smile widens. "My workers are loyal to me, Clay. They tell me everything, or else they know what happens."

"So you tracked Emily and Scarlett's mom down to the river and killed them?"

"Yes. But even though I couldn't find Scarlett and couldn't force that tidbit out of her mother, I knew she was close by. And I couldn't pass up the chance to see my daughter in the flesh after all this time, could I?"

"Shut the hell up," Scarlett says. "And leave Clay out of this."

"Alright. If that's what you want, baby. But I'll need something in return."

Scarlett rolls her eyes with a scoff. "*Fine.* Whatever. But I'll only go with you if it means you won't hurt him."

"Scarlett, no—"

But Conaughey cuts me off. "Let's go. You have three seconds before I change my mind."

Head down, Scarlett takes a tentative step across the dock, in the direction of her father's boat.

Don't do this, I want to tell her, but by the gun aimed on my chest, I know it won't do me any favors.

After three, four steps, Scarlett hesitates, casting a nervous glance over her shoulder. "Wait!" she says. "I forgot something inside. I promise it won't take me long. Just a few seconds to get what I need. And then we're out of here."

"Bullshit," Conaughey says.

"I swear."

Her father sighs, mutters a couple more curses, and says, "Whatever. But make it quick. After a minute, I start shooting. Isn't that right, Clay?"

When he looks my way, flashing that same nauseating grin, it takes everything within me not to break his stare. But I can't show him I'm scared. I can't let him know.

I have to be brave. For Scarlett. For Grandpa. For Ms. Judy.

Fury burns in my stomach at the thought of her falling for Conaughey's charm and smarmy smile, and the terror she must've felt the moment the blade sank between her bones.

I force my own smirk, wondering if he can read my thoughts, knowing all the ways I want to kill him. After all, after everything he's done, isn't that justice? Isn't death what he deserves?

As Scarlett retreats back inside, I can't help but notice the way she hangs back, if only for a second, her fingers gripping the edge of the doorway before stepping inside, as if she's having second thoughts. Her indecisiveness makes a strange feeling flutter in my gut.

Not rage. Not fear. But something else, something like doubt. Like uncertainty.

Even as much as I want to trust her intentions, what is she really capable of in the moment? What will she do when the only way out means going back to *him*?

Ten seconds pass in a flash. I keep track inside my head, wondering what's taking her so long after half a minute's up.

Thirty more seconds before he starts shooting. Thirty more seconds before he pulls the trigger.

I close my eyes. *31…32…33…*

"Come on! I'm not going to give another warning."

Conaughey's voice makes me lose count, beads of sweat popping out along my forehead. Something's not right. It shouldn't be taking her this long.

I blink, the bright sunlight burning my eyes. I stare straight ahead, right at the barrel of the gun, waiting for the flash of the explosion at any moment.

When it comes, I'm nowhere near as prepared as I thought.

Glass shatters behind, something whizzing past my ear and making direct contact with Conaughey's shoulder in the span of a second.

There's a sizzle as metal meets flesh, and a muffled yell emanating from Conaughey's throat as he rocks back on his heels.

When another shot crackles through the air, I fall to my knees, hands over my head.

It's all too sudden, too loud.

Five thundering heartbeats later, a door creaks open and Scarlett steps out into the light.

Her gaze settles on me, crouched down in the Jon boat, watching through the slit between my fingers. Gunshot still ringing in my ears, she nods toward where her father fell only moments before. "I told you I could protect myself," she says.

35

BIG AL

WHEN I BLINK, I notice the .22 rifle still clutched in her hands, fingernails white around the stock. Then the shattered window over her shoulder, the broken panes hanging like jagged teeth. "Did I get him?" she whispers, creeping across the wooden planks and daring a peek below, into the bottom of her father's boat.

From within, I hear a deflated groan, followed by a string of curses. "You shot me! You shot your own father, you crazy b—"

"Shut up! It could've been worse," Scarlett says. She looks at me. "Come on, Clay. Step out of the boat and get up here."

I do as she says. With the gun in her hand, and two slugs inside of her father, adrenaline tingles throughout my body, and I have to cram my shaking hands inside my pockets to keep Scarlett from noticing.

"Are you okay?" I ask, even though she just saved us. Guess I should've known she'd have one last trick up her sleeve.

"Yeah, of course." She leans closer, whispers the rest in my ear. "I'm much better now."

The words make a chill settle inside my bones. The sensation sharpens as Scarlett tucks the .22 rifle to her bicep, pointing the barrel down to where Conaughey lies on his back, clutching a blood-stained hand to his shoulder, specks of red dotting his chin and neck.

His cold eyes stare up at us, a murderous glint behind them. He's still alive, air wheezing through his lips one labored breath at a time.

"Go to hell," he mumbles.

I look away, before the sight of the blood reminds me of Ms. Judy again.

This time, my gaze rests on a shallow, weedy patch of the swamp, where a pair of yellow, reptilian eyes stare back, hovering just above the surface. A rounded snout. Spiky back. Same brown, scaly head.

Big Al.

Scarlett's voice snaps me back to attention. "This is for Mom," she says, tightening her grip around the gun, possibly seconds away from pulling the trigger if I don't stop her in time.

For a second, I consider letting her go through with it, payback for all the women Conaughey's taken through the years and profited off of. Who knows how many of them were forced to sleep with him, even though they might not have been in the right state of mind to provide consent. To me, it's payback for what his actions implicate—that a woman's body is only a tool to use for temporary pleasure and self-fulfillment; as a toy to play with and torture just for the hell of it.

Payback for having the guts to flash that sickening smile, like a narcissistic psychopath who flaunts his charm even when holding a gun to your face. Payback for his victims, like Ms. Judy and Samantha.

But I step in front of her, in front of the weapon, the only way to keep her from following through. "This isn't you, Scarlett," I whisper.

Her upper lip twitches. "He killed my mother."

"I know. And I'm sorry. I'm not even going to pretend like I know how that feels. But you're not a killer. You're not like *him*."

"Get out of my way, Clay," she says, so soft I can barely hear.

"I won't."

"Dammit. Don't make this difficult." Tears form in her eyes, but she blinks them back. "It's not like anyone would ever know."

"Give me the gun and this will all be over. We can get away from here, start over somewhere."

But Scarlett shakes her head. "You don't understand. I can't go back."

My limbs turn to ice as something sounds from behind.

A grunt, followed by the scuffling of feet.

Scarlett's expression morphs from surprise to panic as Conaughey's short, ragged breaths and the soft click of a gun, like the safety being released, register in my mind. Out of the corner of my eye, I catch a flash of metal, a blur of gray.

Conaughey—raising the gun.

Scarlett's hand clamps onto my arm as the world explodes.

A yellow flash. A clap like thunder.

Screaming.

Someone screaming.

The sound of a bullet striking something behind us.

My brain is frozen, frozen in fear.

Another shot, but this time, there is no sound except for an incessant buzzing, like a fly trapped inside my ear.

I shift on my foot too fast, and then I'm falling...f a l l i n g...

Pain shoots through my tailbone as I land on the dock, a puff of air escaping my lips at the sudden impact.

Once my vision focuses, I notice someone falling backward.

Conaughey. Arms flailing overhead as he and his gun tumble over the side of the boat and into the water.

A splash. Another muffled cry.

After that, there is only smoke.

Head spinning, ears ringing, I stand, ignoring the pain coursing through my backside long enough to put one foot in front of the other and stagger forward several steps, scanning the surface for any sign of movement.

Not a second later, Scarlett's beside me, gun still raised to her shoulder, trembling all over. "Are you alright? Are you hurt?"

But I'm only half listening, searching for Conaughey, for his gun, for any hint of danger.

And then I spot the body floating on top of the water, small waves rippling outward from where he fell, drifting ever closer toward the shallow, weedy portion of the swamp.

My heartbeat jackhammers against my ribcage. He's heading straight toward Big Al and her giant underwater nest of babies.

A rounded snout pokes above the surface inches away from Conaughey's motionless figure. The gator's spiky back and dark-striped tail emerge glistening wet from beneath the water. I hold my breath as the creature's mouth opens, pearly-white teeth protruding like small tusks along its strong jaws.

At the last moment, Conaughey stirs, eyes popping open. "What the—"

Big Al's mouth clamps down onto the man's leg with an audible crunch. Like the bleat of a sheep, Conaughey emits a pitiful shriek, before his eyes roll back in his head and the noise dies in his throat.

Mouths agape, both Scarlett and I watch, unable to tear our eyes away from the gruesome scene, like wildlife footage from a National Geographic documentary brought to life.

Then, in a spray of water, the gator disappears beneath the surface, tugging Conaughey's body below until they're only two inky shadows.

Then nothing at all.

"And that," I whisper, "is for Ms. Judy."

36
QUESTIONS

ARRIVING BY BOAT with a game warden or two, the police find us two hours later. After splitting us up into different rooms at the police station with different investigators and probably much different questions, I'm sitting on a wooden bench inside the vacant Sheriff's Department lobby, waiting for Scarlett to be released.

Across the room, a receptionist watches me behind security glass in between occasional sips from her can of Mountain Dew. My tongue is parched, coated with a sour film. I wish I hadn't turned her down thirty minutes ago when she offered me a drink. At the time, I couldn't think of anything but Scarlett and Conaughey and the sheer adrenaline rush of the past few hours, much less a can of soda. Now, it's all I care to think about.

I'm thinking of how much the lobby smells like piss and wet carpet when the front door peels open and a throaty voice calls out, "Clay?"

It's Lynn. Lynn, who reeks of smoke and some cheap, floral

body spray and looks carefully at the receptionist before plopping beside me on the bench. "My God."

"Don't worry. I'm okay."

"Did they catch the bastard who stole your truck?"

"Well, you can say that..."

Lynn stares at me like I've just announced I have cancer. "I told you to be careful," she says. "When the receptionist called to tell me you were at the station—"

"I didn't want you to worry. About the boat, of course."

Lynn rolls her eyes, a trace of a smile on her lips. "Right. The boat."

And then I tell her everything, almost word for word what I told the detectives, starting with the morning I found Samantha's body to this evening, when I called the cops after talking with Conaughey, giving them the exact location of Scarlett's houseboat and urging them to hurry. When Scarlett shot her father and the alligator drug him beneath the surface. When we heard the thrum of a copter's rotors in the distance, and first noticed the boats rounding the bend, surveying the aftermath. When Scarlett looked me in the eyes before the police separated us, letting the words go: *I'm scared, Clay.*

Don't be, I told her. *All you have to do is tell the truth.*

"Did they believe you?" Lynn asks the moment I finish my story. Hearing it out loud, it sounds even more insane than inside my head.

"They had a lot of questions about why I didn't tell anyone about the body. They even threatened me with criminal charges, but it was just to try and scare me to tell the truth. Eventually, they decided my actions made sense and that I wasn't part of a conspiracy."

"What about Conaughey? Did they find his body? Or what's left of it?"

"That's the game warden's job. Guess we'll know in a few days."

"And Scarlett...do you think they'll try and charge her for murder?"

"I'm her only witness. If they don't believe me, then I'm in just as much trouble as she is. They'll treat us both like accomplices in Conaughey's death."

Lynn swats a hand. "You don't have to worry about that. I'll put in a good word with the sheriff first thing tomorrow morning. He's a friend from school, one who'll have no problem listening to what I have to say."

"Thanks. I know it sounds crazy. A lot of it probably doesn't even make much sense." If Dad were here, he'd hug me and tell me I did the best I could, that I'm still learning and that's okay.

Lynn mumbles, "I'm not even going to lie to you, kid. If I was in your shoes, I'd be scared as hell."

Her gaze shifts from my face to the stained carpet beneath our feet, shaking her head as she says, "The worst part is that you didn't feel safe telling me any of it before. Now we're here, and two people are dead. Maybe the rest of them girls could've been found sooner if you'd just told someone."

"Trust me. I know." Head in my hands, I feel like I'm going to be sick. Maybe if I'd told Lynn any day before now, Ms. Judy would still be alive. Maybe I'd still catch her calls at Bart's from time to time and look forward to the excitement on her face whenever I brought her my biggest catch. "And I'm sorry. I'm sorry for not telling you before and not trusting you—"

"Clay," Lynn says. "Look at me."

For a moment, I hesitate, wondering what I'll see when I meet her gaze. Shame. Anger. Or—even worse—disappointment.

But when my stare meets hers, I notice tears forming in the corners of her eyes.

Then again, maybe it's just the light.

She wraps her hand around mine, squeezes. "You might have made a few wrong choices, but you have nothing to be sorry for."

I have everything to be sorry for, I think.

Every right to feel like I'm nothing and never will be. Every right to feel like I'm the guy that's easy for everyone to tolerate but even easier to leave.

Someone with no purpose other than to mess things up and drive a wedge between parents. Someone not even good enough to make people stay.

At the end of all of this, the thing that scares me the most isn't the fact that I could be charged or arrested, but that Scarlett could decide to turn her back on me, on this town, and I wouldn't be able to stop her.

Maybe Lynn's right…maybe it's time I stop feeling sorry for myself and everything that's happened this past week, this past year, and actually strive to be someone better. Someone who doesn't carry the weight of the world on his back or a chip on his shoulder or a grudge against everyone that's left him behind.

Maybe it's time I stop keeping it all in, pretending that everything's okay.

Maybe it's time I let it all go and don't look back.

"I owed it to your dad to keep a close eye on you," Lynn says, letting go of my hand and daring to break the awkward silence. I steal a glance at the receptionist, who's staring straight at us now, not even trying to pretend anymore. I wonder who she thinks Lynn might be. An aunt or distant relative, maybe? My *mom*? "And then, one day, you don't seem like yourself. After everything you've been through, it wouldn't be unusual, but you acted distant. Haunted by something. I've never been a mother and then, out of the blue, I have to make this promise to a dying man that I'll watch after you. To be fair, you haven't made my part any easier.

"However, none of this gives you an excuse. I expect you to be at work on time from here on out. Is that clear?"

"Clear," I say.

"I know it's nowhere near as thrilling as being out there on that river."

"Please. I've had enough excitement for a lifetime."

Lynn nudges my shoulder playfully. "Nah, kid. You're just getting started."

"You think so?"

"I know so. Trust me, it gets better from here. Being a teenager is nothing like it's cracked up to be." She pauses, a glint in her eye. "And I know something else: your dad would be mighty proud."

"Yeah," I whisper. "I think he would."

Lynn looks away for a moment, wiping her eyes with the back of her hand. I can imagine her turning back around, saying, *Dammit, Clay. You've got me crying.*

Instead, she smiles and says, "But not as proud as me."

When Scarlett steps into the lobby, three hours have passed, based on the clock mounted on the wall over my head. Three long hours, evident by the dark creases at the edge of Scarlett's eyes and the sleepy grin on her lips. I have a feeling the effort is more for my benefit than for hers.

"I did it," she says, gripping my hand, the front door to the empty lobby closing behind us as we step out into the night. "I told them the truth."

Lynn left several minutes ago, adamant that I call her the moment I left the station.

But now, heading for my truck parked at the far corner of the lot, I ask, "And did it work?"

Scarlett's grip goes slack, and she tugs away, letting out a shaky breath. Behind her, a streetlight flickers every couple seconds, moths already slamming their furry bodies against the dim bulb. "They took some convincing, but they believed me."

Scarlett explains that the police are aware of these nefarious operations in their jurisdiction and have been working to secure evidence against people like Conaughey for years.

"I gave them the book, too," she says, facing me.

The book—the one we found in a compartment in Conaughey's boat before the police arrived. The list of names scrawled inside, burned into my memory.

Sarah Hayes. Anna Miller. Haleigh Thomas.

Anastasia Abramova. Olga Palahniuk. Svetlana Kuznetsova.

"And? What did they say?"

Scarlett shrugs. "They said they'd take a look at it and get back with me; see if it merits an investigation."

In the meantime, she'll stay with me, since neither of us are allowed to leave town until the case is closed. Since she's eighteen and the State of Florida classifies eighteen-year-olds as adults, Scarlett can technically live on her own. She can leave and not ever have to look back.

But by the defeat in her eyes tonight, I can tell leaving is the furthest thing from her mind. A moment later, when she leans her head against my chest, mumbling "I just want it to be over," all I can do is comfort her.

"I believe you," I say. "About everything."

"You're a good guy, Clay." She blinks away the tears in her eyes, staring up at me. "If only the world could be a little more like you."

"You never told me about your father."

Scarlett shivers beneath her oversized vintage-T. "I was hoping you'd never have to meet him. Thought you'd be safer that way."

In my truck, with the doors closed, we settle in our silence, staring straight ahead through the glass and not speaking a single word. Outside our windows, the night stretches on. Cloudless and vast, speckled with stars. The glowing numbers on the dash read 11:44.

For once, I don't know what happens next. I don't know what the cops will decide in the coming days or who else might come for us.

But does anything else really matter, except knowing that Scarlett's safe?

Seeming to read my mind, Scarlett turns to me in the passenger seat. "What now?" she asks.

I place a finger beneath her chin, pulling her closer until our lips brush. "Anything you want."

Scarlett blushes, and then she kisses me. Her lips are soft and startling and perfect all at once. "Let's get outta here, Clay."

37

RADIO SILENCE

Two Weeks Later

IT DOESN'T TAKE long before the news ends up making the front page of *The River Gazette*, below the large headline *Teens Lead Police to Human Trafficking Ring: Fifteen Missing Women Found.*

Grandpa studies it in a corner table at Delton Café, holding a magnifying glass an inch above the small black print. "Well, I'll be. Those kids deserve a gold medal. Or two weeks with no chores."

Scarlett winks across the table at me, over the rim of her milk glass.

"Yeah," I say. "Guess so."

The café is abuzz with the news, evident in the pointed stares in our direction and whispers behind palms the moment we walked through the door. It's also the best news to happen in this area in years, except for that time Ms. Beulah's kittens were rescued from her she-shed fire by the Delton fire department.

Catching a glimpse of the newspaper's front cover, Dinah

trots over to our table, refilling both mine and Grandpa's tea glasses. "Sure are some special kids," she says, flashing a sneaky smile at us before Grandpa can notice.

Even if our names aren't printed once in the nearly six-hundred word story in order to ensure our safety, word travels quick, and gossip even faster. I guess it didn't take much head scratching for the old men to link my strange behavior the day I darted from Lucy's kitchen to something as significant as uncovering the leaders behind a human trafficking ring, who'd been operating in plain sight for years.

"Here. Let me see that for a minute."

Taking the paper from Grandpa, I skim the several columns of black text until I find the list of women's names that have been safely located, six of which were listed in the pages of that notebook buried beneath the floorboards in a houseboat along Dead River.

Sarah Hayes. Anna Miller. Haleigh Thomas...

I hand the paper back, grinning ear to ear.

I can't stop smiling, even when the conversation shifts and Grandpa's moved on to something else. When I look at Scarlett, I notice she can't either.

Five minutes into my 9 o'clock shift, still full from breakfast, the phone rings.

Lynn beats me to it. "Bart's," she huffs. "What can I help you with?"

One hand on the receiver, the other nervously twitching by her side, as if in need of a cigarette, she points to me and mouths, "It's for you."

Ms. Judy.

It's always my first thought whenever that phone rings. In some way, I almost expect to hear her voice whenever I pick up, to hear her say my name just to make sure she's talking to the right person.

But instead of shrill and squeaky, the voice that answers is quieter, more monotone.

"Clay?" Hearing my name spoken from a stranger's mouth gives me a fleeting second of panic.

It could be anyone. Bart himself, or even Conaughey, back from the dead.

When the person speaks again, their voice is faint yet familiar. Hushed, like the words are meant to be secret. "Baby? Is that you?"

The woman's tone is what gives it away, that slight quiver at the end of each word. It's a voice I haven't heard in years; one I forgot I remembered until now.

My head spins as I lick my lips, whisper, "Mom?"

I will a glance in Lynn's direction, but she's disappeared down the small hallway leading to the office.

Of course it's not her. I should know better. She hasn't bothered to call in eleven years. After all this time, why now?

"I read about you in the paper," she says, as if reading my thoughts. "That was a real good thing you did, son."

"How did you know it was me? My name wasn't printed."

"I can't reveal my sources," she chuckles, even if it's not the answer I want to hear. Words that mean nothing since she's been absent from my life longer than she was a part of it.

"I don't believe you."

"Well, you know I wouldn't lie?"

She says it like it's a question. Like she doesn't quite know if it's a lie herself.

How would I know if she's telling the truth? To me, she's more of a stranger than someone I used to live with; a woman who's eleven years too late.

"What do you want?" I don't even try to disguise my annoyance; there are plenty of reasons she's the last person I want to be talking to right now.

"I just wanted to hear your voice," she says.

"Really? That's it?" I could hang up right this moment and be perfectly satisfied with never speaking another word to her again. After all the pain she's caused me and Dad, it wouldn't even hurt my feelings.

"Can't that be enough?"

"It won't ever be enough." I shake my head, swallowing back the hard lump in my throat. *Don't you dare cry. Don't you dare—*

"How'd you know I work here?" I ask, even if there's still a thousand better questions I could ask instead. *Why did you leave us? Where have you been? Who have you been?*

"Your dad," she says. "He kept in touch."

"Oh, was that before or after the cancer diagnosis?"

"Clay. Please don't be mad..."

"Why? Give me one good reason."

I pace the aisles, back and forth, staring at the vinyl-tile floor.

"I know how it looks. It makes me seem like a terrible human and an even worse mother—"

"No, not terrible. *Selfish* is more like it."

That startles her into silence, but not for long enough. "I'll never forgive myself. For any of it. But sometimes, you have to decide what matters most. And it was a decision I had to make."

"Look, I don't know what you want or why you suddenly seem to care so much, but I actually have work to do—"

"I don't expect you to understand," she cuts in. "I didn't even expect you to make it this long without hanging up. I just saw that article in the paper and realized it's been too long since I heard your voice. Guess I wanted to let you know that I haven't forgotten. Make sure you were okay."

"After eleven years you call to make sure I'm *okay*?"

Then it hits me. My mother called for a truce, a lame attempt to make her presence known the instant I've done something worth recognizing. And now she wants credit. And if not that, then a way back into my life, seeing a way to take advantage of me now that Dad's gone.

"I don't expect you to understand," she says again, voice barely above a whisper.

"Understand what? That you care more about yourself than your own family?" The words spew out of me, pent-up for too long. "Dad's diagnosed with cancer, Grandpa starts forgetting my name, and where are you? On a cruise ship with your new fiancé? Chasing waterfalls across the country? One phone call doesn't forgive the last decade, Mom. The point is, when I needed you most, you weren't here at all."

"Don't think for *one second* that I wanted this," she says, with the first tinge of emotion since our conversation started. Pathetic, I know, but it almost makes me want to believe her. Almost. "If things were any different, maybe I could've stayed, but the fact of the matter is that it would have been much worse for the both of you if I had."

"How? How could it have been any worse?"

"It's a long story."

"I have time."

"Thought you had work to do?"

"Yeah, well it's not every day your mother calls out of the blue after a decade of radio silence."

"Then I'm sorry. Sorry I bothered you."

I wait for her to speak again, but there's nothing…no indication that she hasn't already ended the call. "Wait! Don't hang up. I want to know something."

A beat of silence, the only sound the rapid thrum of my heartbeat, and then: "If it'll make you feel better, then I might can tell you."

"Why didn't you come back? Not even when Dad was sick?"

She answers faster than expected, almost as if she practiced the lie before calling. "Because I didn't know."

"But you're the one who said he still kept in touch…"

"Not about that. Not about his health. He was a private person and we grew apart after so many years."

"So how'd you know when he—"

"Please. You don't have to say it. It was a couple weeks before I heard the news from a close friend. I know it might not be what you want to hear, but there are a lot of things about my life now that prevent me from staying up to date."

"Yeah? Like what?"

"I'm guessing your dad never told you."

"Told me what?"

If I was annoyed before, now I'm angry. All this back-and-forth, chasing rabbits. Dodging the truth with more questions and quite possibly more lies.

"Not now, Clay. Not like this," she whispers.

"Why? Why does it have to be a secret?"

"Because there are terrible people who might make sure I never hear from you again."

"Are you in trouble? Is someone threatening you—?"

She doesn't answer. Not right away. When her voice finally returns, it's quieter than ever. "I want you to write down this number. No more questions. Just do it. The area code is ..."

As she rattles off the digits, I hurry to the counter, scrambling for a pen. Writing the numbers on the back of my hand, I wonder why she's suddenly gone silent.

In the background, echoing through the faintest of static, there's a noise like that of a door slamming. Then a voice so deep it rattles my skull.

"Natasha? What are you doing?"

"Mom? Can you still hear me?" I ask, heart thumping.

"Sorry. I have to go," she says. "I love you."

With a click, she's gone, leaving me with more questions than I started with.

38

TATTOO

A COUPLE DAYS AFTER the conversation with my mother, my second random call of the week comes from a man who introduces himself as Ms. Judy's attorney.

"I found a note in Ms. Judy's file. Your name was written on it, along with a few instructions. In case something happened to her, she wanted you to be the one in charge of sorting through her household possessions." His chipper voice fades to a business-like tone. "Just a heads up, son, but I've read her will and she's going to leave the house to you. It'll probably take several months to get that settled, but in the meantime, feel free to get started and see what needs to be kept or thrown out."

Now, using a key from the attorney's office, I step inside Ms. Judy's house, police tape still strung across a hallway door.

Staring into the living room, at the clutter of Sudoku books, crossword puzzles, and food wrappers, I let out a sigh. I don't even know where to start. And the worst part is—where I should be honored that she'd even consider leaving her house in my name to begin with—my heart's just not in it.

She's gone now, and nothing worth keeping or throwing out will change that.

A floral-covered photo album catches my eye from the center of the coffee table. Black-and-white photos fill the insides, save for a colored one or two, crammed behind plastic sheaths.

One photo in particular catches my eye. Using two fingers, I pinch a pointy edge of the photograph and work it out into the light. It's an image of a woman and a little girl, whose small arms are wrapped around the woman's waist, cheek pressed against her side on the steps of a narrow front porch.

It's the same photo from that shack along Dead River, yet nowhere near as grainy or blotchy in appearance.

Several words are written across the back. *Dead River. Summer of '86.*

Another one, at the top of the next page, five words scribbled in the same distinct black scrawl on the opposite side: *Mile Lake. Summer of '87.*

In the background, the lake sparkles in the sun, three figures dressed in overalls holding hands at the water's edge. The same woman and little girl.

Samantha, I tell myself, whose hand-in-hand with another female of the same stature. I take in Samantha's tiny, scrunched-up nose, pointed chin, and that dimple, digging into the left side of her face. Then my gaze flicks to the little girl standing beside her, grin so forced it seems unnecessary. Like she's only smiling because it's expected. Like she's seen so much that showing even the slightest emotion hurts.

Who are you? And how did you know Samantha?

The woman—pixie-cut hair, slender waist, wide hips—stands slightly hunched, just like she used to when standing from her recliner too fast or waving at me from her front porch in passing. Her features are whisper-thin, lips narrow and eyebrows sparse, even then. But it's the smile that gives it away. One I'd know anywhere.

It's Ms. Judy. A much younger version of her anyway. Gripping Samantha's hand and staring straight into the camera lens.

The puzzle piece slides into place in my mind. It's the reason she purposely called Scarlett by her mother's name and seemed to be lying when I'd asked her if the girl looked familiar. Quite possibly the same reason she left me this house in the first place.

But why? Was it because she didn't want to die without leaving someone else to discover her secret? Was it because she was afraid the pictures might end up in the wrong hands or thrown away by the police?

Or was it simply because she thought I should know the truth?

Maybe she believed I earned that right. Maybe, after showing her Scarlett's hideout, she knew I needed the history of these photos to better understand the present.

My mind races back to the pushpins in Grandpa's map.

One pinned at Mile Lake. Another at Dead River.

Both locations aren't connected by tragedy as I previously thought.

They're both landmarks connected by lost girls— Samantha; that girl with the lazy grin—and Grandpa and Ms. Judy's secrets.

I remember Ms. Judy hunched beneath her plastic windbreaker in the boat that day. Her words: *As long as we stay away from Dead River. Brings back too many memories.*

At the time, I assumed something bad had taken place there. But the real reason she wanted to steer clear of the area was because of her own past. Perhaps the sight of it would have brought back a time when Grandpa still had his memory and Samantha was still around. Perhaps the recollection of events would've been too painful, too sharp after so many years.

Still, I can't help but wonder what might've happened after those pictures were taken; why Grandpa and Ms. Judy decided to call it quits and why Samantha ended up veering apart from them.

My fingers brush against the second little girl's bare feet in the photo of Mile Lake. There's something about her posture and that hesitant smile that looks familiar. Was she a prisoner too?

Soon, I move on to the other pages, searching for answers within every face, every black-and-white image. Most of them are meaningless—a blurry angle of someone's face, someone's lawn, someone's station wagon. None offering any clues behind Ms. Judy's secret past or the other two young, pale-faced girls in the pictures taken along the river.

Maybe that's all I'm supposed to know. Maybe that's all there ever was to it.

Grandpa found Samantha screaming for her mama one night at Mile Lake.

Thirty-seven years later, she's found strangled to death on the edge of the bank.

I flip another page. What am I missing? What happened in the time after 1986?

Then I find it, another photo of Samantha and her friend running barefoot through the creek, clad in skin-tight bathing suits, hair swishing around their faces. The image is taken mid-shot, at just the right angle for me to catch a sliver of the unnamed girl's left shoulder, where an inky shape stains her skin.

It's nothing and everything all at once.

I sit it beside me on the couch with the other photos of the girls, knee bouncing as I comb through the album, hairs rising on the nape of my neck.

There's one of Ms. Judy, possibly on the same day, darting after them in a sleeveless shirt and a pair of cut-off jeans, sneaking a quick glance over her shoulder back at the camera or at Grandpa, in the process of snapping the photo.

My gaze locks onto her shoulder.

Something dark and cone-shaped takes up a wide portion of her skin, completely visible in the camera's angle.

It's a tattoo. A sketch of something geometric and parallel, the only two visible sides shaped like triangles, which rise to a small peak, like the tip of a mountain.

Something Scarlett once said comes back to me: *Maybe you don't know her as well as you think.*

I slam the book closed. Put my head in my hands, taking in shallow breaths.

A tattoo. Ms. Judy had a tattoo.

Which is almost as absurd as admitting the truth: the tattoo was shaped like a pyramid.

39

FUTURE

AFTER RETURNING HOME from Ms. Judy's, I find Grandpa kicked back in his recliner, watching *Swamp People*.

The living room hums with silence. Grandpa prefers to keep the TV muted with subtitles flashing across the bottom of the screen, though I doubt he ever reads them. He's seen every episode of the show, but he can't remember that he has, so it's like he's watching it for the first time.

"Shoot 'em, Clint! Shoot 'em!" Grandpa grips the arms of his lounger. "Don't let 'em get away!"

I smile to myself as I take a seat on the sofa, watching Grandpa grow frustrated.

He sighs and rubs his forehead. "Look at this mess, Jason. These boys don't know what they're doing. That's no way to catch a gator."

"They'll get it. They always do."

"Yeah, well they're making my blood pressure go up. They better get after it." His gaze meets mine. "Me and Judy caught a gator once. I ever tell you 'bout that?"

Judy. The name from his mouth makes my heart race. I haven't heard him mention her in a long time. In fact, the last time I asked him about her, he couldn't remember who she was.

"No. You haven't."

He turns back to the screen. "There ya go, Clint! Now that's a nice-sized one."

"Grandpa. What about Ms. Judy?"

"Huh?" He looks at me and blinks once, twice. "What was I saying?"

"Ms. Judy. You were telling me about when you and her—"

"That's right!" Grandpa slaps his forehead. "I was telling you about what she did for a living, wasn't I? It was real dangerous business."

"What kind of business?"

Grandpa leans forward in his recliner, looking around the living room, as if we aren't the only ones here. Lowering his voice, he says, "Well, before I knew her, she used to be involved in a human trafficking ring. But a woman got her out of it, smuggled her to the river. After that, Judy started helping other girls escape the same ring she did."

Just like Scarlett's mom. But with the realization comes more questions, a million of them it seems. I need to know the answers, before Grandpa loses his train of thought and I'm left with nothing.

"How did you know what Ms. Judy was doing? And why would she tell you? Wouldn't that only put you in danger?"

"She had to, Jason," Grandpa says. "Especially once I found that little girl at Mile Lake one night. She knew I'd stumbled upon her secret, and she had no choice but to tell me who those girls were and where they came from. Once I knew, I couldn't just walk away. It was too dangerous."

Did Dad know? I wonder. *Did Ms. Judy and Grandpa tell him about this?*

Grandpa continues: "When we were teenagers, we'd spend all our time on the river, making forts, spotting for swimming holes. I thought she was normal, like me. The strangest thing about her was her tattoo. I thought it was cool; I didn't know any girls our age with a tattoo."

"Did she tell you how she got it?"

He shakes his head. "She didn't like to talk about it; I could tell it upset her. But once I found that girl at Mile Lake years later, screaming her head off, I was real spooked. Of course, I couldn't keep something like that to myself. I told Judy about it, and that's when she told me the truth. I couldn't believe it. I thought I knew her!"

"You helped her raise these girls?"

"Yep. It was the least I could do."

What he said a couple weeks ago comes to mind: *The bad men are coming, Jason.*

"Were you ever scared the men from the ring would track Ms. Judy down? Figure out where the girls went and get rid of them?"

Grandpa's eyes widen. "You bet I was scared! Told Judy we had to keep the girls hidden. At least until we knew it was safe."

Then, a little softer, he adds, "Those people will be back one day, just wait and see. And when they get here, I'll be ready for 'em." Grandpa looks around, his eyes combing the floor on either side of his recliner. "Where's my gun? You seen it anywhere?"

"What about the girls, Grandpa?" He looks up at me. "Why did they leave? Where did they go?"

What happened in the time after 1986? After that photo taken at Dead River?

Grandpa leans back, crosses his arms, and stares up at the ceiling, like he's trying to remember. I'm about to ask him the question again, convinced he's lost his train of thought, when he says, "Well, Samantha left the first chance she got. She wanted to see the world, to explore. That young'un could never keep still." He chuckles.

I think about the photo of Ms. Judy with Samantha and another pale-faced child. "What about the other girl? What happened to her? Do you know her name?"

Grandpa's throat gurgles, as if he's trying to form the words. "I...I don't...can't..."

Then he starts to cry. His shoulders shake, and large tears roll down his cheeks.

I stand from the sofa and rush over to him, rubbing his back. "Grandpa, it's all right. We don't have to talk about it anymore. Don't cry."

"I loved her," he sniffles. "I loved her so much."

I wrap my arms around him, feel his body shake with sobs. "It's okay. Shhh. It's okay."

After a minute, he stops crying and trembling. "She gave me the best years," he whispers. "She was my entire world. But we grew apart, weren't the same people as when we were kids. When the girls left and moved on, there was no reason for us to be together anymore. Things change. People change."

Ms. Judy. He's talking about Ms. Judy.

"I thought I'd never get over her, Jason. When she left, it damn well broke me." A tear drips from his chin onto his blue denim shirt. "But I guess there ain't no need to be sad. I've still got something important, don't I?"

"What's that?" I ask, letting him go.

He looks up at me. "I've still got you. I don't know what I'd do without you." I hug him again, and this time, he hugs me back. "Son, how about bringing me my tea? Mouth's getting dry."

"Alright." I wipe a tear from his cheek. "Anything for you, Grandpa."

I go and pour him a glass of iced tea from a pitcher in the fridge. When I return, he's kicked back in his recliner again, the tears gone from his eyes. He stares at the TV, quiet and still.

"Here you go." I hold the drink out to him.

"Well, isn't that nice. How'd you know I was getting thirsty?"

I smile, and he takes the glass.

After a few sips, he motions toward the TV, says, "Look at this mess, Jason. These boys are embarrassing themselves. That's no way to catch a gator."

"They'll get it. Half of it's just for show. Got to keep the viewers entertained somehow."

"That reminds me"—Grandpa places the drink on the coffee table next to his recliner—"of when me and Judy caught that gator at Mile Lake. I ever tell you 'bout that?"

"No."

"Well, it was me, Judy, Samantha, and…and…that other girl. For the life of me, I can't seem to remember—"

"Grandpa?"

"Yes, Jason?"

"The girls from the ring. Do you know who I'm talking about?"

His white eyebrows twitch. He doesn't say anything.

I try anyway, knowing I won't have his attention for long. "Why did Ms. Judy bring them to the river and not somewhere else?"

"Because." Grandpa grins, a sneaky glint in his eyes. "There's a lot you can keep hidden out there."

Then he winks.

Twilight settles over the swamp, bleeding hues of ashy gray, cool orange, and wisps of pink through the treetops in the western sky.

Scarlett and I sit on the edge of the dock. There's no sound out here, other than the background noise of crickets and the hum of mosquitoes in the distance.

We've been talking for hours. Mainly about school and possible career options and our lives in the real world, away from the marsh.

Scarlett's going back to get her GED in the fall, while I finish up the few classes I have left in order to graduate. After that, everything seems a little murky. Scarlett's talked about becoming a psychologist, so she can help others with their escape from tragedy or abuse. In the meantime, I'm still putting in my hours at Bart's, keeping up with my fishing business on the side, which has steadily picked up since everyone knows who I am now. That's thanks to Lynn's television debut on the Channel 7 news, where an anchor asked her about the bodies discovered along the river not far from her store. She hadn't hesitated to drop my name either, telling everyone that her employee helped solve the biggest crime in the panhandle, so I guess everyone knows now.

The future still scares me a little, talks of college degrees and scholarships making me more anxious than I'd like to admit. I'm perfectly content with staying right where I am for the time being, the busy world outside of the swamp a far cry from the safety and seclusion and quaintness of our lives here, now that no one is after us.

After all, the river's in my blood. It's all I've ever known. It's here where I feel the closest to Dad and Grandpa, even Ms. Judy.

Speaking of, the old woman even bequeathed me a pontoon boat in her will, according to her attorney. He said it was her idea to give me the boat as a head start in my new venture. This includes guided tours of the river swamp, which I hope to make a career. Thanks to Ms. Judy, it can happen right after high school. Saving money for a boat won't even be an issue.

Scarlett's voice interrupts my thought. "You think it's a coincidence that Ms. Judy smuggled trafficked girls to the river like Mama did?"

"If I believed in coincidences, maybe," I say. "But it's more of a tradition, don't you think?"

Earlier today, I showed Scarlett the pictures—the ones of her mother and Ms. Judy and the other little girl, hurrying up the stream. Most importantly, I'd shown her the secret emblem on Ms. Judy's shoulder.

At first, Scarlett had been just as startled as I was, but the more we thought about things, the more the truth became clear. Particularly why Ms. Judy sounded so ominous when I asked her if she would believe what Scarlett had been through. *I believe I would. More than you know.*

Something tells me that once Ms. Judy recognized Scarlett the day I took her to Lost Lake, she knew history had repeated itself, and that Samantha had taken her daughter to the river, where she would be safe. Just like Ms. Judy had done for her.

Watch out for that girl, she told me, as if she knew exactly who Scarlett was.

I wonder if her response to finding the game camera was built out of her paranoia, her need to be cautious and cover up her tracks, just in case the men from the ring could trace the camera back to her. I wonder if she ever got over the fear that one day, the people from her past would find her. It makes me contemplate whether women like her ever truly escape the ring. Scarlett's mom chose to get involved with it again later in life. Ultimately, both her and Ms. Judy were killed by the ring, depending on how you look at it. In that case, I can't help but ask myself: *Were they ever free?*

"I know what you're thinking, but we have to leave this alone," Scarlett says. "We're not telling the police anything about her. Ms. Judy's reputation deserves peace. She'd want that."

"But what if there's more out there that police could link to Ms. Judy's past? Maybe more lost girls that haven't been found?"

Scarlett doesn't answer for a while, dipping a toe in the water, and watching tiny ripples form across the surface. "Do you love me?"

The question catches me off guard. Even though I haven't yet said it aloud, I know the answer. "Of course I do."

Scarlett nods. "Then you'll leave this alone." Tugging on a strand of hair, she says, "In some ways, Ms. Judy was kind of like the grandmother I never knew. I mean, she practically saved my mother's life."

I mull over the possibilities. "How do you feel about moving into her house?"

Scarlett's eyes widen. "Are *we* moving in together? Like a couple?"

"Sure. We'll see where it goes." I lean my head against her shoulder, feeling safer than I have in weeks. "You know I'll still have to check on Grandpa."

Scarlett wipes her face a second later and I pull back, staring into her teary eyes. "What's wrong?"

"I never thought I'd be lucky enough to have something like this," Scarlett chokes out.

I wrap my arms around her, kissing her temple. "Neither did I."

I think back to those nights before I found her, lying awake in bed, lonely and wanting nothing more than to leave this town behind.

Now, with Scarlett by my side, I want nothing more than to stay.

For once, I don't have to worry about the things beyond my control or the feelings that still surge within my gut on occasion, searing and raw. I don't have to worry because Scarlett's experienced the same and because she bothered to stay when no one else would.

I'll never have to face it alone.

Epilogue

"**H**OW DOES ONE woman end up with so much crap?"

Scarlett props the bulging garbage bag against the coffee table, wiping sweat from her brow. The air is stuffy and filled with dust motes, swirling all around us in the light sneaking in through the parted drapes. After countless bags and trips to the overflowing garbage can at the end of the drive, we've finally finished cleaning out Ms. Judy's living room.

"Only five rooms to go," I groan.

After that, the chore will turn into a renovation project—new carpet, a new smell, and a fresh coat of paint on the walls.

"I'm thinking we go several shades darker," Scarlett says, sweeping a hand around the living room, indicating the pale-pink interior. "You know, like a Pepto Bismol color."

"You do have the best ideas," I wince, stifling a gag.

Scarlett nudges me in the shoulder, mid-laugh. I'm reaching out for the garbage bag when she asks, "What's that? Some girl's number you forgot to wash away?"

Her voice is joking, yet still laced with suspicion. Out of instinct, I rub my fingers across the faded ink on the back of my hand, hoping to wipe away any trace of the numbers from my skin, but it's no use. The digits are still there, completely readable. No matter how hard I scrub them or how many showers I take, I just can't seem to get rid of them.

"No. Just some customer I forgot to call back. He was in a hurry."

I search for any indication on Scarlett's face that suggests she doesn't believe me. Thankfully, with a glimmer of a smile, she lets it go. "Of course. Just giving you a hard time."

I stare at the ink, remembering Mom's sketchy silence that day over the phone and that booming voice in the background, as if she'd been caught talking to someone forbidden. The way she dodged my questions, failing to provide any sort of concrete answer as to where she'd been for the past eleven years.

"Actually, do you mind if I call them back real quick? It'll only take a minute."

Scarlett shakes her head, holding out a hand for the garbage bag. "Here. Let me take that to the end of the drive. If you're not finished by the time I've made it back, I'm moving on to the storage closet. Probably be there all day at this rate."

Slinging the bag over her shoulder with a grunt, Scarlett staggers out the door, leaving it cracked behind her.

Just as she slips from sight, I dig the phone from my pocket and type in the number.

Someone picks up on the third ring.

"Hello? Can I help you?" a gruff voice answers. Definitely not Mom.

"Hi. May I speak with Natasha?"

"Who is this?"

"Clayton Thomas. Her son."

For a moment, there's no sound. "Listen," he says, voice nowhere near as kind, "I've already told you. Leave us alone. It's been thirty-five years. Stop digging salt in the wound and let my wife and I heal. Try and move on for Christ's sake."

I hold the phone away from my ear, the man's voice suddenly too heated, too loud. It almost sounds like the same voice I heard in the background that day, but with even more passion and a slight quiver to his tone. This can't be the same guy, the one who caused Mom to end the call on a whim and go silent.

"I'm sorry. I must have the wrong number. May I ask who's speaking?"

"Where are you reporting from? How much did they pay you?"

"*Pay* me? I just want to speak with my mother. She gave me this number herself."

"No," the stranger says. "That's not possible."

"Look, I don't know what this is, but I really need to talk to her—"

"You can't." He lets out a shaky breath. "She's been missing since 1987."

I bite back a chuckle. "Am I being pranked or something? This has to be a joke."

I move to the closest window, watching Scarlett struggle across the lawn through a slit in the curtains, now pulling the bag across the ground, teeth gritted.

Screw it. She needs help. I'm about to end the call when the man speaks up. "Sir? You still there?"

"How do you know Natasha?"

"What do you mean, *how do I know Natasha?* She's my daughter."

The words startle me into silence. He's Natasha's father? If so, why haven't I heard of him before? Does that make him my *grandpa*?

I'm beginning to wonder if we're even talking about the same person. No way my mother's been missing since 1987. I lived with her for six years. Wouldn't I have known?

It's probably a big misunderstanding. Either she gave me the wrong number, or I misheard her.

But then I think of the photo in Ms. Judy's album and the words written across the back: *Mile Lake. Summer of '87.*

Samantha and that other girl—the one with the tired eyes and the forced grin.

When the man speaks again, I'm hunched over the coffee table, rifling through the photo album.

"Hello? Can you still hear me? I think you're cutting out."

There. A flash of small bare feet; overalls, hanging off a diminutive frame.

I look into the girl's eyes and all I see is my mother staring back at me.

The realization jogs my memory...the way Mom buried herself beneath makeup those mornings before work, until she was unrecognizable, even to me; the way she used to tuck me into bed late at night, whispering tales of stowaways on a train, heading north; the forlorn look she got whenever I caught her staring out our front porch window, tendrils of smoke rising from a coffee cup.

Not because Mom yearned for something different—a way out of this life, away from *us*—but because she knew staying would only put us in more danger. Because she knew the only way to protect me, Dad, and possibly even Ms. Judy, was to leave, before her past caught up with her.

Her heels, click-clacking down the walk; the car door slamming, engine revving.

This entire time, it was all for *me*.

Mom used to be a prisoner, but Ms. Judy smuggled her to the river, saving her life. Depending on how old Mom was at the time she was rescued, it's possible she wouldn't have remembered her parents and Ms. Judy wouldn't have known who to return her to. Only, how did Mom get caught up in the ring again? How am I supposed to know where to look for her? Is that why she left me this number? So I would know the truth?

"Listen," I whisper, fingers tightening around the phone, "I've got to go. But can I call you again?"

The man sighs. After a pause: "Sure."

And then I end the call, slumping to the floor.

Dad knew; of course he did. He fell in love with one of the girls Ms. Judy saved. It makes perfect sense now why he hid Mom's letters from me. If I wrote her back, if I'd sent just one note with my zip code, they would've known where to find me.

A door closes in the hall, gentle as a whisper. Not a second later, a figure appears in the entranceway to the living room.

It's Scarlett, both brows raised. "Are you okay?"

"Yeah, of course," I say, rising to my feet. My head spins. I close my eyes. "Just feeling a little tired."

"Listen," she says, blowing out a sigh. "Not that it has anything to do with that number on the back of your hand, but I've been thinking."

Silence.

When I open my eyes, I notice Scarlett's gone still. She's staring at the photo...the one still gripped in my hand. "What's that?"

"It's nothing," I blurt, stuffing the picture in my back pocket before she can get a better look.

"Anyway," Scarlett says, "if we're going to move in together and we're really, *really* serious about this, then we need to be honest about things from this point on. To be fair, I just want to make sure we can trust each other now." Scarlett steps forward, her arms slipping around my waist. Her breath tickles my ear. "No more secrets?"

"Of course," I whisper back. Thankfully, with her head pressed to my chest, she doesn't notice the way my arms clasp behind her back to keep them from trembling or my pinpoint stare on the photo album resting atop the coffee table, which I'd forgotten to close. "No more secrets."

Except for one.

ACKNOWLEDGEMENTS

I started writing this one in March 2020, at the beginning of lockdown. During such a hellish time, the Choctawhatchee River and this book were my escape.

First, I must thank my parents, not only for purchasing the Jon boat that led to many river excursions, but for their constant love and support.

Much thanks to my beta readers for their invaluable feedback and encouragement: Hope Allen, Tammy Cosson, Olivia Garrett, Quinton Johnson, Tara Manson, and Kristen Nelson. I must also thank my Creative Writing classmates at Northwest Florida State College for critiquing the first two chapters of *Dead River* and lending their generous and kind words, especially Belle, Ethan, and Fiona.

Tremendous thanks to Gillian French; the fact that one of my favorite authors read my book still doesn't seem real. Your feedback was crucial to the development of this book. Thank you for your kindness, your encouragement, and for your front cover quote.

Thanks to: my editor, Josh Vogt, for making this book better and stronger than it was before; Amanda Bosenberg Photography for shooting on location at the Choctawhatchee River; Damonza for the brilliant cover and interior formatting; and Watt Key for turning me into a reader and for inspiring me to write, even now.

A special thanks to my Creative Writing professor, Dr. Hunt—one of the greatest educators I've ever known. Thank you for teaching me that words are powerful, words are important. However, I could never put into words how much you meant to so many people, especially me. I miss you. You left us too soon.

Finally, I must thank you for reading this book. I hope you enjoyed it, and I can't wait for you to see what's coming next.

ABOUT THE AUTHOR

McCaid Paul is the author of *The Forgotten Headline*, *Secret Trust*, and others. Three of his poems and a personal essay were published in the 2022 literature journal, *Blackwater Review*, of Northwest Florida State College. When he is not daydreaming about new stories, you can find him drinking too much coffee and sweet tea, taking long hikes in the woods, or fishing for hours at a time on the Choctawhatchee. To learn more, visit him online at mccaidpaulbooks.com or on Instagram and Facebook @ mccaidpaul.

Ingram Content Group UK Ltd.
Milton Keynes UK
UKHW011945080523
421401UK00004B/332